THE MAN WHO UNDERSTOOD WOMEN

BY LEONARD MERRICK

THE POSITION OF PEGGY
CONRAD IN QUEST OF HIS YOUTH
THE MAN WHO UNDERSTOOD WOMEN:
   STORIES
WHISPERS ABOUT WOMEN : STORIES
LYNCH'S DAUGHTER
THE MAN WHO WAS GOOD
THIS STAGE OF FOOLS
CYNTHIA
ONE MAN'S VIEW
THE ACTOR MANAGER
THE WORLDLINGS
WHEN LOVE FLIES OUT O' THE WINDOW
THE QUAINT COMPANIONS

Several of Mr. Merrick's books are at present unpublished in America. Mitchell Kennerley will publish new volumes from time to time.

THE MAN
WHO UNDERSTOOD
WOMEN

BY

LEONARD MERRICK

MITCHELL KENNERLEY
NEW YORK AND LONDON
MCMXI

THE MAN WHO UNDERSTOOD WOMEN

I

THE MAN WHO UNDERSTOOD WOMEN

"Our bitterest remorse is not for our sins, but for our stupidities."—Excerpt from Wendover's new novel.

NOTHING had delighted Wendover so much when his first book appeared as some reviewer's reference to "the author's knowledge of women." He was then six or seven-and-twenty, and the compliment uplifted him the more because he had long regretted violently that he knew even less of women than do most young men. The thought of women fascinated him. He yearned to captivate them, to pass lightly from one love affair to another, to have the right to call himself "blasé." Alas! a few dances in the small provincial town that he had left when he was eighteen comprised nearly all his sentimental experiences; during his years of struggle in London he had been so abominably hard up that lodging-house keepers and barmaids were almost the only women he addressed, and as his beverage

1

was "a glass of bitter," the barmaids had been strictly commercial.

To be told that he understood women enraptured him. "Instinct!" he said to himself. "Now and then a man is born who knows the feminine mind intuitively." And in his next book there was an abundance of his fanciful psychology. Denied companionship with women, he revelled in writing about them, and drew from the pages in which he posed as their delineator, something of the exultation that he would have derived from being their lover. There were even pages after which he felt sated with conquest. At these times nothing accorded with his mood so well as to parade the Park and pretend to himself that the sight of the most attractive of the women bored him.

But as loneliness really cried within him pathetically, he had an adventure, culminating in marriage with a shop assistant who glanced at him one evening in Oxford Street. After marriage they found as little of an agreeable nature to say to each other as might have been expected, so a couple of years later they separated, and the ex-shop hand went to reside with a widowed sister, who "made up ladies' own materials" at Crouch End.

Gradually he came to be accepted at his own valuation, to be pronounced one of the few gifted men from whom the feminine soul held no secrets. Then when he was close on forty, a novel that he published hit the popular taste, and he began to make a very respectable income.

Now, for the first time, he had opportunities for meeting the class of women that he had been writing about, and he found to his consternation, that they failed to recognise him as an affinity after all. They were very amiable, but, like the farmer with the claret, he "never got any forrader." He perceived that his profundities were thought tedious, and that his attentions were thought raw. It was a sickening admission for an authority on women to have to make, but when he tried to flirt he felt shy.

At last he decided that all the women that he knew were too frivolous to appeal to a man of intellect, and that their company wearied him unutterably.

But, though he had reached middle-age, he had never as yet been really in love.

In the autumn of his forty-second year—few people judged him to be so much—he removed to Paris. Some months afterwards, in the interests of a novel that he had begun, he deserted his hotel in the Rue d'Antin for a pension on the left bank. This establishment, which was supported chiefly by English and American girls studying art, supplied the "colour" that he needed for his earlier chapters; and it was here that he made the acquaintance of Miss Searle.

Miss Searle was about six-and-twenty, bohemian,

and ambitious beyond her talents. Such pensions
abound in girls who are more or less bohemian, and
ambitious beyond their talents, but Rhoda Searle
was noteworthy—her face stirred the imagination,
she had realised that she would never paint, and
the free-and-easy intercourse of the Latin Quarter
had wholly unfitted her for the prim provincialism
to which she must return in England.

"My father was a parson," she told Wendover
once, as they smoked cigarettes together after dinner. "I had hard work to convince him that English art schools weren't the apex, but he gave in at
last and let me come here. It was Paradise! My
home was in Beckenhampton. Do you know it?
It's one of the dreariest holes in the kingdom. I
used to go over to stay with him twice a year. I
was very fond of my father, but I can't tell you how
terrible those visits became to me, how I had to
suppress myself, and how the drab women and
stupid young men used to stare at me—as if I were
a strange animal, or something improper; in places
like Beckenhampton they say 'Paris' in the same kind
of voice that they say 'Hell.' I suppose I'm a bohemian by instinct, for even now that I know I
should never make an artist, my horror isn't so
much the loss of my hopes as the loss of my freedom, my—my identity; I am never to be natural
any more! After I leave here I am to go on sup-
pressing myself till the day I die! Sometimes I shall

be able to shut myself up and howl—that's all I've got to look forward to."

"What are you going to do?" asked Wendover, looking sympathetic, and thinking pleasurably that he had found a good character to put into his book.

"I am going back," she said, "a shining example of the folly of being discontented with district-visiting and Church bazaars! I go back a failure for Beckenhampton to moralise over. My old schoolmistress has asked me to stay with her while I 'look round'—you see, I've spent all my money, and I must find a situation. If the Beckenhampton parents don't regard me as too immoral, it is just possible she may employ me in the school to 'teach drawing'—unless I try to teach it! Then I suppose I shall be called a 'revolutionary,' and be dismissed." She contemplated the shabby little salon thoughtfully, and lit another cigarette. "From the Boule' Mich' to a boarding school! It'll be a change! I wonder if it will be safe to smoke there if I keep my bedroom window open wide?"

Yes, it would be as great a change as was conceivable, and Rhoda Searle was the most interesting figure in the house to Wendover. She was going to England in a month's time—there was no reason why she should not go at once, save that she had enough money to postpone the evil day—and during this valedictory month, she and he talked of their "friendship." In the tortuous streets off the

Boulevard, she introduced him to humble restaurants, where the dinners were sometimes amazingly good at ridiculously low prices. Together they made little excursions, and pretended to scribble or sketch in the woods—looking at each other, however, most of the time; and then at evening there was an inn to be sought, and the moon would rise sooner than the "friends"; and in the moonlight, when they returned to Paris and the pension, sentiment would constrain their tones.

It was all quite innocent, but to the last degree unwise. The ex-shop assistant still throve decorously in Crouch End on his allowance, and Wendover should have seen that he was acting unfairly towards Miss Searle. To do him justice, he didn't see it—he had confided the story of his marriage to her, and it did not enter into his thoughts that she might care for him seriously notwithstanding; his experiences had given him no cause to esteem himself dangerous, and the lover who has never received favours is, in practice, always modest, though in aspirations he may be Juanesque. The suitor of quick perceptions has been made by other women, as everybody but the least sophisticated of débutantes knows.

But if he did not dream that he might trouble the peace of Miss Searle, he was perpetually conscious that he had disturbed his own. A month's daily companionship with a temperament, plus a fascina-

ting face, would be dangerous to any man—to Wendover it was fatal. His thoughts turned no longer
to liaisons with duchesses; his work, itself, was sec-
ondary to Rhoda Searle. Silly fellow as he appears,
the emotions wakened in him were no less genuine
than if he had combined all the noble qualities with
which he invested the heroes of his books. Besides,
most people would appear silly in a description which
dealt only with their weaknesses. Wendover loved,
and he cursed the tie that prevented his asking the
girl to be his wife. How happy he might have
been!

He had feared that the last evening would be a
melancholy one, but it was gay—the greater part of
it was gay, at any rate. As soon as the door slammed behind them he saw that she had resolved to
keep the thought of the morrow's journey in the
background, to help him to turn the farewell into
a fête. Her laughing caution was unnecessary, her
voice, her eyes had given him the cue—her journey
was to be undertaken in the distant future, life was
delicious, and they were out to enjoy themselves!
He had proposed dining at Armenonville—it wasn't
the Paris that she had known, but champagne and
fashion seemed the right thing to-night; and no
fiacre had ever sped so blithely before, never had
the Bois been so enchanting, and never had another
girl been such joyous company. After dinner, the
Ambassadeurs! The programme? They didn't

listen to much of it, they were chattering all the
time. It was only when the lamps died out that he
heard a sigh; it was only when the lamps died out
that the morning train, and the good-bye, and the
blank beginning of the afterwards, seemed to him
so horribly near.

The little salon was half dark when they reached
the pension; everybody else had gone to bed. Wendover turned up the light, and, though she said it
was too late to sit down, they stood talking by the
mantelpiece. "You've given me a heavenly memory for the end," she told him; "thanks so much!
I shall be thinking of it at this time to-morrow."

"So shall I," said Wendover.

She took off her hat, and pulled her hair right
before the mirror. "Shall you?"

"Will you write to me?"

"Yes, if you'd like me to."

"I'd more than like it—I shall look forward to
your letters tremendously."

"There won't be much to say in them."

"They'll be from *you*. . . . I wish you weren't
going."

She raised her eyes to him. "Why?" she asked.

Wendover kept silent a moment—it was the
hardest thing that he had done in his life. If he
answered, "Because I love you," he felt that he
would be a cad. Besides, she must know very well
that he loved her—what good would it do to tell

her so?—doubtless she had repented her question in the moment of putting it! Yes, he would be a cad to confess to her—she would think less of him for it. He would choose the beau rôle—and she would always remember that, when he might have spoilt their last scene together and pained her, he had been strong, heroic!

"We've been such pals," he said. That she mightn't underrate the heroism, he turned aside, as the noble fellow in books does when he is struggling.

After a pause, she murmured blankly. "It's time I said 'good-night.'"

She went to him and gave him her hand. Her clasp was fervent—it was encouraging to feel that she was grateful! Her gaze held him, and her eyes were wide, dark, troubled; he was sure that she was sorry for him.

"Good-night, my dear," said Wendover, still as brave as the fellow in the books. And when he had watched her go up the stairs—when she had turned again, with that look in her eyes, and turned away—he went back to the salon and was wretched beyond words to tell, for a fool may love as deeply as the wisest.

This was really their "good-bye"—in the morning the claims on her were many, and he was not the only one who drove to the station with her.

When she had been gone between two and three weeks, he received the promised letter. It told him little but that she was "the new drawing mistress"; of her thoughts, her attitude towards her new life, it said nothing. He replied promptly, questioning her, but she wrote no more, and not the least of his regrets was the thought that she had dismissed him from her mind so easily.

He did not remain much longer in the pension, its associations hurt him too much. A sandy-haired girl, with no eyelashes and red ears, occupied the seat that had been Rhoda's at the table, and the newcomer's unconcerned possession of it stabbed him at every meal. Having taken precautions against letters for him going astray, he returned to the hotel, and there month after month he plodded at his book, and tried to forget.

Nearly a year had gone by when he stood again on the deck of a Channel boat. He had not spared himself, and the novel was finished, and he was satisfied with it; but he was as much in love as he had been on the morning when he watched a train steam from the Gare St. Lazare. As he paced the deck he thought of Rhoda all the time; it excited him that he was going to England, he might chance to see her—he might even run down to Beckenhampton for a day or two? It would make the situation harder to bear afterwards, of course, but——

He looked up "Beckenhampton" in the Railway Guide often during the next few days. The distance

between them was marvellously short—the knowledge that an hour and a half's journey could yield
her face to him again had a touch of the magical
in it. An hour and a half from Hades to Olympus!
The longing fevered him; he threw some things into
a bag pell-mell one morning and caught the 10.15.

"The George Hotel!"—and from the hotel he
directed the driver to the school. The little town
was grey and drear; he pitied her acutely as he
gazed about him from the fly. He understood how
her spirit must beat itself against the bars, he realised what her arrival must have meant to her—
behind one of the windows of this prison she had
sat looking back upon her yesterday! How the
year must have changed her! he wondered if she
still smiled. The fly jolted into the narrow High
Street—and he saw her coming out of the post
office.

Yes, she still smiled—the smile that irradiated
her face, and made him forget everything else!
They stood outside the post office together, clasping
hands once more.

"You! what are you doing here?" she cried.

"I was just going to see you, I've just come from
the station. How are you? You look very well."

"I'm all right. Are you back for good?"

"Yes, I left Paris a few days ago."

"Did you stay on at the pension?"

"Oh no, I gave that up soon after you went."

"You've finished your book, eh?"

"How did you know?"

"I saw something about it in a paper. And how's Paris? I dream I'm back sometimes."

"Paris is just the same."

"I suppose you never saw anything of the others afterwards—Kitty Owen, or the McAllister girl?"

"No, I never came across any of them—I was working very hard. Well? Tell me things; what's the news? You're still at the school, then?"

"No."

"No? Aren't you? I was on my way there. What are you doing?"

"I'm married."

The blood sank from his cheeks. "Married?"

"I've been married four months."

A woman came between them to post a letter, and he was grateful for the interruption. "Let me congratulate you!"

"Thanks. My husband's a solicitor here. . . . You'll come and see us?"

"I'm afraid—I should have been delighted, of course, but I have to be in town again this evening."

"We'd better move—we're in everybody's way," she said. "Will you walk on with me? When does the book come out?"

"In a few weeks' time—I'll send a copy to you."

"Really? It would be very good of you. I've

often looked at the book columns to see if it was published."

"Have you? I was afraid you'd forgotten all about me. . . . You—you might have written again, you promised to write!"

"I know."

"Why didn't you?"

"What was the good?"

"It would have made me happier. I missed you frightfully. I—I think that was why I left the pension, I couldn't stand it when you'd gone. . . . Well, are *you* happy?"

"Oh, I suppose so."

"I'm glad."

"So you won't come and see us?"

"It's impossible, I'm sorry to say. . . . As a matter of fact, I didn't mean to see you again at all."

"That's a pretty compliment!"

"Ah, you know what I mean—it seemed better that I shouldn't. But . . . I think I'm glad I did. I don't know! I've wondered sometimes whether you understood. . . . We shan't meet any more, and I should like you to know——"

"Don't!" she exclaimed, quickly, "For heaven's sake!"

"I must," said Wendover—"I loved you dearly!"

They had walked some yards before she answered; her voice was a whisper: "What's the use

of saying that to me now?" The bitterness of suffering was in the words—they flared the truth on
him, the brutal, annihilating truth.

"My God!" he faltered, "would it have been any
use *then?*"

Her face was colourless. She didn't speak.

"Rhoda, did you care? If—if I had asked you
to stay with me, would you have stayed?"

"I don't know."

"Tell me."

"Yes, then, I *would* have stayed!" she said
hoarsely. "Whom should I have hurt? I was
alone, I had no one to study but myself. I wanted
you to ask me. Stayed? I'd have thanked God
if you had spoken! You were blind, you *wouldn't*
see. And now, when it's too late, you come and
say it!"

"I wanted to be straight to you," he groaned. "I
sacrificed my happiness to be straight to you—it
was damnably hard to do."

"I know. But I didn't want sacrifices—I wanted
love. . . . Oh, it's no good our talking about
it!" She stopped, and sighed. "We shall both
get over it, I suppose."

"*Is* it too late?" pleaded Wendover brokenly.

"Quite! Things aren't the same; last year I was
free to do as I liked. I have no conventions, but I
have a conscience—there's my husband to consider
now, and—and more, too! I shouldn't be contented

like that to-day—I should have injured others. You and I let our chance slide, and we shall never get it back. . . . Smile, and say something about nothing —there are people who know me coming along."

And he did not sleep at the George after all; in the next train that left for Euston, a grey-faced man sat with wide eyes, cursing his own obtuseness. Nor has he met her since. There is, of course, a brighter side to the history—although Rhoda is unhappy, she is happier than she would have remained with Wendover when the gilt was off the gingerbread; and though Wendover will never forget her, he cherishes her memory with more tenderness than he would have continued to cherish the girl.

But neither she nor he recognises this, and in Wendover's latest work, one may see the line that has been quoted: "Our bitterest remorse is not for our sins, but for our stupidities."

The reception of the novel was most flattering, and as usual the author's "insight into the mind of Woman" has been pronounced "remarkable."

II

THE SUICIDES IN THE RUE SOMBRE

HAVING bought the rope, Tournicquot wondered where he should hang himself. The lath-and-plaster ceiling of his room might decline to support him, and while the streets were populous a lamp-post was out of the question. As he roamed on, he reflected that a pan of charcoal would have been more convenient after all; but the coil of rope in the doorway of a shop had lured his fancy, and now it would be laughable to throw it away.

Tournicquot was much averse from being laughed at in private life—perhaps because Fate had willed that he should be laughed at so much in his public capacity at Le Jardin Extérieur. Could he have had his way, indeed, Tournicquot would have been a great tragedian, instead of a little droll, whose portraits, with a bright red nose and a scarlet wig, grimaced on the kiosks; and he resolved that, at any rate, the element of humour should not mar his suicide.

As to the motive for his death, it was as romantic as his heart desired. He adored "La Belle Lu-

crèce," the fascinating Snake Charmer, and somewhere in the background the artiste had a husband.
Little the audience at Le Jardin Extérieur suspected
the passion that devoured their grotesque comedian
while he cut his capers, and turned love to ridicule;
little they divined the pathos of a situation which
condemned him behind the scenes to whisper the
most sentimental assurances of devotion when dis-
figured by a flaming wig and a nose that was daubed
vermilion! How nearly it has been said, One half
of the world does not know how the other half
loves!

But such incongruities would distress Tournicquot
no more—to-day he was to die; he had worn his
chess-board trousers and his little green coat for the
last time; for the last time had the relentless virtue
of Lucrèce driven him to despair. When he was
discovered inanimate, hanging to a beam, nothing
comic about him, perhaps the world would admit
that his soul had been solemn, though his "line of
business" had been funny; perhaps Lucrèce would
even drop warm tears upon his tomb!

It was early in the evening. Dusk was gathering
over Paris; the promise of dinner was in the breeze.
The white glare of electric globes began to flood
the boulevards, and before the cafés, waiters bustled
among the tables, bearing the vermouth and absinthe of the hour. Instinctively shunning the more
frequented thoroughfares, Tournicquot wandered,

plunged in reverie, until he perceived that he had reached a neighbourhood which was unknown to him—that he stood at the corner of a street which bore the name "Rue Sombre." Opposite, one of the houses was being rebuilt, and as he gazed at it—this skeleton of a home in which the workmen's hammers were silenced for the night—Tournicquot recognised that his journey was at an end. Here, he could not doubt that he would find the last, grim hospitality that he sought. The house had no door to bar his entrance, but—as if in omen—above the gap where a door had been, the sinister number "13" was still to be discerned. He cast a glance over his shoulder, and, grasping the rope with a firm hand, crept inside.

It was dark within, so dark that at first he could discern nothing but the gleam of bare walls. He stole along the passage, and, mounting a flight of steps on which his feet sprung mournful echoes, proceeded stealthily towards an apartment on the first floor. At this point the darkness became impenetrable, for the persiennes had been closed, and in order to make his arrangements, it was necessary that he should have a light. He paused, fumbling in his pocket; and then, with his next step, blundered against a body, which swung from the contact, like a human being suspended in mid-air.

Tournicquot leapt backwards in terror. A cold sweat bespangled him, and for some seconds he shook so violently that he was unable to strike a match. At last, when he accomplished it, he beheld an apparently dead man hanging by a rope in the doorway.

"Oh, mon Dieu!" gasped Tournicquot. And the thudding of his heart seemed to resound through the deserted house.

Humanity impelled him to rescue the poor wretch, if it was still to be done. Shuddering, he whipped out his knife, and sawed at the cord desperately. The cord was stout, and the blade of the knife but small; an eternity seemed to pass while he sawed in the darkness. Presently one of the strands gave way. He set his teeth and pressed harder, and harder yet. Suddenly the rope yielded and the body fell to the ground. Tournicquot threw himself beside it, tearing open the collar, and using frantic efforts to restore animation. There was no result. He persevered, but the body lay perfectly inert. He began to reflect that it was his duty to inform the police of the discovery, and he asked himself how he should account for his presence on the scene. Just as he was considering this, he felt the stir of life. As if by a miracle the man groaned.

"Courage, my poor fellow!" panted Tournicquot. "Courage—all is well!"

The man groaned again; and after an appalling silence, during which Tournicquot began to tremble for his fate anew, asked feebly, "Where am I?"

"You would have hanged yourself," explained Tournicquot. "Thanks to Heaven, I arrived in time to save your life!"

In the darkness they could not see each other, but he felt for the man's hand and pressed it warmly. To his consternation, he received, for response, a thump in the chest.

"Mon Dieu, what an infernal cheek!" croaked the man. "So you have cut me down? You meddlesome idiot, by what right did you poke your nose into my affairs, hein?"

Dismay held Tournicquot dumb.

"Hein?" wheezed the man; "what concern was it of yours, if you please? Never in my life before have I met with such a piece of presumption!"

"My poor friend," stammered Tournicquot, "you do not know what you say—you are not yourself! By-and-by, you will be grateful, you will fall on your knees and bless me."

"By-and-by I shall punch you in the eye," returned the man, "just as soon as I am feeling better! What have you done to my collar, too? I declare you have played the devil with me!" His annoyance rose. "Who are you, and what were you doing here, anyhow? You are a trespasser—I shall give you in charge."

"Come, come," said Tournicquot, conciliatingly, "if your misfortunes are more than you can bear, I regret that I was obliged to save you; but, after all, there is no need to make such a grievance of it; you can hang yourself another day."

"And why should I be put to the trouble twice?" grumbled the other. "Do you figure yourself that it is agreeable to hang? I passed a very bad time, I can assure you! If you had experienced it, you would not talk so lightly about 'another day.' The more I think of your impudent interference, the more it vexes me. And how dark it is! Get up and light the candle—it gives me the hump here."

"I have no candle, I have no candle," babbled Tournicquot. "I do not carry candles in my pocket."

"There is a bit on the mantelpiece," replied the man, angrily; "I saw it when I came in. Go and feel for it—hunt about! Do not keep me lying here in the dark—the least you can do is to make me as comfortable as you can!"

Tournicquot, not a little perturbed by the threat of assault, groped obediently; but the room appeared to be of the dimensions of a park, and he arrived at the candle stump only after a prolonged excursion. The flame revealed to him a man of about his own age, who leant against the wall regarding him with indignant eyes. Revealed, also, was the coil of rope that the comedian had brought for his own use; and the man pointed to it.

"What is that? It was not here just now."

"It belongs to me," admitted Tourniquot, nervously.

"I see that it belongs to you. Why do you visit an empty house with a coil of rope, hein? I should like to understand that! . . . Upon my life, you were here on the same business as myself! Now, if this does not pass all forbearance! You come to commit suicide, and yet you have the effrontery to put a stop to mine!"

"Well," exclaimed Tournicquot, "I obeyed an impulse of pity! It is true that I came to destroy myself, for I am the most miserable of men; but I was so much affected by the sight of your sufferings that temporarily I forgot my own."

"That is a lie, for I was not suffering—I was not conscious when you came in. However, you have some pretty moments in front of you, so we will say no more! When you feel yourself drop, it will be diabolical, I promise you; the hair stands erect on the head, and each spot of blood in the veins congeals to a separate icicle! It is true that the drop itself is swift, but the clutch of the rope, as you kick in the air, is hardly less atrocious. Do not be encouraged by the delusion that the matter is instantaneous. Time mocks you, and a second holds the sensations of a quarter-of-an-hour. What has forced you to it? We need not stand on ceremony with each other, hein?"

"I have resolved to die because life is torture," said Tournicquot, on whom these details had made an unfavourable impression.

"The same with me! A woman, of course?"

"Yes," sighed Tournicquot, "a woman!"

"Is there no other remedy? Cannot you desert her?"

"Desert her? I pine for her embrace!"

"Hein?"

"She will not have anything to do with me!"

"Comment? Then it is love with you?"

"What else? An eternal passion!"

"Oh, mon Dieu, I took it for granted that you were married! But this is droll. *You* would die because you cannot get hold of a woman, and *I* because I cannot get rid of one. We should talk, we two. Can you give me a cigarette?"

"With pleasure, monsieur," responded Tournicquot, producing a packet. "I, also, will take one—my last!"

"If I expressed myself hastily just now," said his companion, refastening his collar, "I shall apologise—no doubt your interference was well meant, though I do not pretend to approve it. Let us dismiss the incident; you have behaved tactlessly, and I, on my side, have perhaps resented your error with too much warmth. Well, it is finished! While the candle burns, let us exchange more amicable views. Is my cravat straight? It astonishes me to hear that love can drive a man to such despair. I, too, have loved, but never to the length of the rope. There are plenty of women in Paris—if one has no

heart, there is always another. I am far from pro-
posing to frustrate your project, holding as I do
that a man's suicide is an intimate matter in which
'rescue' is a name given by busybodies to a gross
impertinence; but as you have not begun the job, I
will confess that I think you are being rash."

"I have considered," replied Tournicquot, "I have
considered attentively. There is no alternative, I
assure you."

"I would make another attempt to persuade the
lady—I swear I would make another attempt! You
are not a bad-looking fellow. What is her objection
to you?"

"It is not that she objects to me—on the contrary. But she is a woman of high principle, and
she has a husband who is devoted to her—she will
not break his heart. It is like that."

"Young?"

"No more than thirty."

"And beautiful?"

"With a beauty like an angel's! She has a dim-
ple in her right cheek when she smiles that drives
one to distraction."

"Myself, I have no weakness for dimples; but
every man to his taste—there is no arguing about
these things. What a combination—young, lovely,
virtuous! And I make you a bet the oaf of a husband does not appreciate her! Is it not always so?
Now *I*—but of course I married foolishly, I mar-

ried an artiste. If I had my time again I would choose in preference any sempstress. The artistes are for applause, for bouquets, for little dinners, but not for marriage."

"I cannot agree with you," said Tournicquot, with some hauteur. "Your experience may have been unfortunate, but the theatre contains women quite as noble as any other sphere. In proof of it, the lady I adore is an artiste herself!"

"Really—is it so? Would it be indiscreet to ask her name?"

"There are things that one does not tell."

"Perfectly! But as a matter of interest? There is nothing derogatory to her in what you say—quite the reverse."

"True! Well, the reason for reticence is removed! She is known as 'La Belle Lucrèce.'"

"*Hein?*" ejaculated the other, jumping.

"What ails you?"

"She is my wife!"

"Your wife? Impossible!"

"I tell you I am married to her—she is 'Madame Béguinet.'"

"Mon Dieu!" faltered Tournicquot, aghast; "what have I done!"

"So? . . . You are her lover?"

"Never has she encouraged me—recall what I said! There are no grounds for jealousy—am I

not about to die because she spurns me? I swear to
you——"

"You mistake my emotion—why should I be
jealous? Not at all—I am only amazed. She
thinks I am devoted to her? Ho, ho! Not at all!
You see my 'devotion' by the fact that I am about
to hang myself rather than live with her. And *you,*
you cannot bear to live because you adore her!
Actually, you 'adore' her! Is it not inexplicable?
Oh, there is certainly the finger of Providence in
this meeting! . . . Wait, we must discuss—we
should come to each other's aid! . . . Give me
another cigarette."

Some seconds passed while they smoked in silent
meditation.

"Listen," resumed M. Béguinet; "in order to
clear up this complication, a perfect candour is required on both sides. Alors, as to your views, is
it that you aspire to marry Madame? I do not wish
to appear exigent, but in the position that I occupy
you will realise that it is my duty to make the most
favourable arrangements that I can for her. Now
open your heart to me; speak frankly!"

"It is difficult for me to express myself without
restraint to you, monsieur," said Tournicquot, "because circumstances cause me to regard you as a
grievance. To answer you with all the delicacy
possible, I will say that if I had cut you down five
minutes later, life would be a fairer thing to me."

"Good," said M. Béguinet, "we make progress! Your income? Does it suffice to support her in the style to which she is accustomed? What may your occupation be?"

"I am in Madame's own profession—I, too, am an artiste."

"So much the more congenial! I foresee a joyous union. Come, we go famously! Your line of business—snakes, ventriloquism, performing-rabbits, what is it?"

"My name is 'Tournicquot,'" responded the comedian, with dignity. "All is said!"

"A-ah! Is it so? Now I understand why your voice has been puzzling me! Monsieur Tournicquot, I am enchanted to make your acquaintance. I declare the matter arranges itself! I shall tell you what we will do. Hitherto I have had no choice between residing with Madame and committing suicide, because my affairs have not prospered, and —though my pride has revolted—her salary has been essential for my maintenance. Now the happy medium jumps to the eyes; for you, for me, for her the bright sunshine streams! I shall efface myself; I shall go to a distant land—say, Belgium—and you shall make me a snug allowance. Have no misgiving; crown her with blossoms, lead her to the altar, and rest tranquil—I shall never re-appear. Do not figure yourself that I shall enter like the villain at the Ambigu and menace the blissful home.

Not at all! I myself may even re-marry, who
knows? Indeed, should you offer me an allowance
adequate for a family man, I will undertake to re-
marry—I have always inclined towards speculation.
That will shut my mouth, hein? I could threaten
nothing, even if I had a base nature, for I, also,
shall have committed bigamy. Suicide, bigamy, I
would commit anything rather than live with Lucrèce!"

"But Madame's consent must be gained," demurred Tournicquot; "you overlook the fact that
Madame must consent. It is a fact that I do not
understand why she should have any consideration
for you, but if she continues to harp upon her 'duty,'
what then?"

"Do you not tell me that her only objection to
your suit has been her fear that she would break my
heart? What an hallucination! I shall approach
the subject with tact, with the utmost delicacy. I
shall intimate to her that to ensure her happiness I
am willing to sacrifice myself. Should she hesitate,
I shall demand to sacrifice myself! Rest assured
that if she regards you with the favour that you
believe, your troubles are at an end—the barrier
removes itself, and you join hands. . . The candle is going out! Shall we depart?"

"I perceive no reason why we should remain; in
truth, we might have got out of it sooner."

"You are right! a café will be more cheerful.

Suppose we take a bottle of wine together; how does it strike you? If you insist, I will be your guest; if not——"

"Ah, monsieur, you will allow me the pleasure," murmured Tournicquot.

"Well, well," said Béguinet, "you must have your way! . . . Your rope you have no use for, hein —we shall leave it?"

"But certainly! Why should I burden myself?"

"The occasion has passed, true. Good! Come, my comrade, let us descend!"

Who shall read the future? Awhile ago they had been strangers, neither intending to quit the house alive; now the pair issued from it jauntily, arm in arm! Both were in high spirits, and by the time the lamps of a café gave them welcome, and the wine gurgled gaily into the glasses, they pledged each other with a sentiment no less than fraternal.

"How I rejoice that I have met you!" exclaimed Béguinet. "To your marriage, mon vieux; to your joy! Fill up, again a glass!—there are plenty of bottles in the cellar. Mon Dieu, you are my pre-server—I must embrace you! Never till now have I felt such affection for a man! This evening all was black to me, I despaired, my heart was as heavy as a cannon-ball—and suddenly the world is bright! Roses bloom before my feet, and the little larks are singing in the sky. I dance, I skip! How beautiful, how sublime is friendship!—better than riches, than

youth, than the love of woman; riches melt, youth
flies, woman snores. But friendship is—— Again
a glass! It goes well, this wine. Let us have a
lobster! I swear I have an appetite; they make one
peckish, these suicides, n'est-ce-pas? I shall not be
formal—if you consider it your treat, you shall pay.
A lobster and another bottle? At your expense or
mine?"

"Ah, the bill all in one!" declared Tournicquot.

"Well, well," said Béguinet, "you must have your
way! What a happy man I am! Already I feel
twenty years younger. You would not believe what
I have suffered! My agonies would fill a book.
Really! By nature I am domesticated; but my home
is impossible—I shudder when I enter it. It is
only in a restaurant that I see a clean tablecloth.
Absolutely! I pig! All Lucrèce thinks about is
frivolity."

"No, no," demurred Tournicquot; "to that I cannot agree."

"What do you know? You 'cannot agree'! You
have seen her when she is laced in her stage costume,
when she prinks and prattles, with the paint, and
the powder, and her best corset on. It is I who am
'behind the scenes,' mon ami, not you! I see her
dirty peignoir and her curl rags. At four o'clock in
the afternoon! Every day! You 'cannot agree'!"

"Curl rags?" faltered Tournicquot.

"But certainly! I tell you I am of a gentle disposition; I am most tolerant of women's failings; it says much that I would have hanged myself rather than remain with a woman. Her untidiness is not all; her toilette at home revolts my sensibilities, but —well, one cannot have everything, and her salary is substantial; I have closed my eyes to the curl rags. However, snakes are more serious."

"Snakes!" ejaculated Tournicquot.

"Naturally! The beasts must live, do they not support us? But 'everything in its place' is my own motto; the motto of my wife—'All over the place.' Her serpents have shortened my life, word of honour!—they wander where they will. I never lay my head beside those curl rags of hers without anticipating a cobra-de-capello under the bolster. It is not everybody's money! Lucrèce has no objection to them; well, it is very courageous—very fortunate, since snakes are her profession—but *I,* I was not brought up to snakes; I am not at my ease in a Zoological Gardens."

"It is natural."

"Is it not? I desire to explain myself to you, you understand; are we not as brothers? Oh, I realise well that when one loves a woman one always thinks that the faults are with the husband; believe me, I have had much to justify my attitude. Snakes, dirt, furies, what a ménage!"

"Furies?" gasped Tournicquot.

"I am an honest man," affirmed Béguinet, drain-

ing another bumper; "I shall not say to you 'I have
no blemish, I am perfect.' Not at all! Without
doubt, I have occasionally expressed myself to Lucrèce with more candour than courtesy. Such things
happen. But——," he refilled his glass, and sighed
pathetically, "but to every citizen, whatever his position—whether his affairs may have prospered or
not—his wife owes respect. Hein? She should not
throw the ragoût at him. She should not menace
him with snakes." He wept. "My friend, you will
admit that it is not genteel to coerce a husband with
deadly reptiles?"

Tournicquot had turned very pale. He signed to
the waiter for the bill, and when it was discharged,
sat regarding his companion with round eyes. At
last, clearing his throat, he said nervously:

"After all, do you know—now one comes to think
it over—I am not sure, upon my honour, that our
arrangement is feasible?"

"What?" exclaimed Béguinet, with a violent start.
"Not feasible? How is that, pray? Because I have
opened my heart to you, do you back out? Oh,
what treachery! Never will I believe that you could
be capable of it!"

"However, it is a fact. On consideration, I shall
not rob you of her."

"Base fellow! You take advantage of my confidence. A contract is a contract!"

"No," stammered Tournicquot, "I shall be a man

and live my love down.   Monsieur, I have the honour to wish you 'Good-night.' "

"Hi, stop!" cried Béguinet, infuriated.   "What
then is to become of *me?*   Insolent poltroon—you
have even destroyed my rope!"

III

LITTLE-FLOWER-OF-THE-WOOD

JANIAUD used to lie abed all day and drink absinthe
all night. When he contrived to write his poetry is
a mystery. But he did write it, and he might have
written other things, too, if he had had the will. It
was once suggested that his paramount duty was to
publish a history of modern Paris, for the man was
an Encyclopædia of unsuspected facts. Since he can
never publish it now, however, I am free to tell the
story of the Loup Blanc as he told it to an English
editor and me one night on the terrace of the Loup
Blanc itself. It befell thus:

When we entered that shabby little Montmartre
restaurant, Janiaud chanced to be seated at a table
in a corner of the ground-floor room, sipping his
favourite stimulant. He was deplorably dirty, and
resembled a scarecrow, and the English editor
looked nervous when I offered an introduction. Still,
Janiaud was Janiaud! The offer was accepted, and
Janiaud discoursed in his native tongue.

At midnight the Editor ordered supper. Being
unfamiliar with the Loup Blanc in those days, I said

34

that I would drink beer. Janiaud smiled sardonic-
ally, and the waiter surprised us with the infor-
mation that beer could not be supplied.

"What?"

"After midnight, nothing but champagne," he
answered.

"Really? Well, let us go somewhere else," I
proposed.

But the Editor would not hear of that. He had
a princely soul, and, besides, he was "doing Paris."

"All the same, what does it mean?" he inquired
of Janiaud.

Janiaud blew smoke rings. "It is the rule. During the evening the bock drinker is welcomed here
as elsewhere; but at midnight—well, you will see
what you will see!"

And we saw very soon. The bourgeoisie of
Montmartre had straggled out while we talked, and
in a little while the restaurant was crowded with a
rackety crew who had driven up in cabs. Everybody but ourselves was in evening dress. Where
the coppers had been counted carefully, gold was
scattered. A space was cleared for dancing, and
Mlle. Nan Joliquette, from Olympia, obliged the
company with her latest comic song.

The Editor was interested. "It is a queer change,
though! Has it always been like this?"

"Ask Janiaud," I said: "*I* don't know."

"Oh, not at all," replied Janiaud; "no, indeed,

it was not always like this! The Loup Blanc used to be as quiet at midnight as at any other hour. But it became celebrated as a supper-place; and now it is quite the thing for the ardent spirits, with money, to come here and kick up their heels until five in the morning."

"Curious, how such customs originate!" remarked the Editor. "Here we have a restaurant which is out of the way, which is the reverse of luxurious, and which, for all that, seems to be a gold mine to the proprietor. Look at him! Look at his white waistcoat and his massive watch-chain, his air of prosperity! The man's a millionaire in miniature."

"How did he come to rake it in like this, Janiaud —you know everything?" I said.

The poet stroked his beard, and glanced at his empty glass. The Editor raised the bottle.

"I cannot talk on Clicquot!" demurred Janiaud. "If you insist, I will take another absinthe. Doubtless they will allow it in the circumstances. Sst, Adolphe!" The waiter whisked over to us. "Monsieur pays for champagne, but I prefer absinthe. There is no law against that, hein?"

Adolphe smiled tolerantly.

"Shall we sit outside?" suggested the Editor. "What do you think? It's getting rather riotous in here, isn't it?"

So we moved on to the terrace, and waited while Janiaud prepared his poison.

"It is a coincidence that you have asked me for the history of the Loup Blanc to-night," he began, after a gulp; "if you had asked for it two days earlier, the climax would have been missing. The story completed itself yesterday, and I happened to be here, and saw the end.

"Listen! Dupont—the proprietor whom Monsieur has just admired—used to be chef to a family on the Boulevard Haussmann. He had a very fair salary, and probably he would have remained in the situation till now but for the fact that he fell in love with the parlour-maid. She was a sprightly little flirt, with ambitions, and she accepted him only on condition that they should withdraw from domestic service and start a business of their own. Dupont was of a cautious temperament; he would have preferred to jog along with some family where a married couple were acceptable in the capacities of chef and housekeeper. Still, he consented; and, with what they had saved between them, they took over this little restaurant—where Monsieur the Editor has treated me with such regal magnificence! It was not they who christened it—it was called 'Le Loup Blanc' already; how it obtained its name is also very interesting, but I have always avoided digressions in my work—that is one of the first principles of the literary art." He swallowed some more absinthe.

"They took the establishment over, and they conducted it on the lines of their predecessor—they provided a table d'hôte déjeuner at one franc fifty, and a table d'hôte dinner at two francs. These are side-shows of the Loup Blanc to-day, but, in the period of which I speak, they were all that it had to say for itself—they were its foundation, and its cupola! When I had two francs to spare, I used to dine here myself.

"Well, the profits were not dazzling. And after marriage the little parlour-maid developed extravagant tastes. She had a passion for theatres. I, Janiaud, have nothing to say against theatres, excepting that the managers have never put on my dramas, but in the wife of a struggling restaurateur a craze for play-going is not to be encouraged. Monsieur will agree? Also, Madame had a fondness for dress. She did little behind the counter but display new ribbons and trinkets. She was very stupid at giving change—and always made the mistake on the wrong side for Dupont. At last he had to employ a cousin of his own as dame-de-comptoir. The expenses had increased, and the returns remained the same. In fine, Dupont was in difficulties; the Loup Blanc was on its last legs.

"Listen! There was at that time a dancer called 'Little-Flower-of-the-Wood.' She was very chic, very popular. She had her appartement in the Avenue Wagram, she drove to the stage-doors in her coupé, her photographs were sold like confetti at a

carnival. Well, one afternoon, when Dupont's reflections were oscillating between the bankruptcy
court and the Morgue, he was stupefied to receive
a message from her—she bade him reserve a table
for herself and some friends for supper that night!

"Dupont could scarcely credit his ears. He told
his wife that a practical joker must be larking with
him. He declared that he would take no notice of
the message, that he was not such an ass as to
be duped by it. Finally, he proposed to telegraph
to Little-Flower-of-the-Wood, inquiring if it was
genuine.

"Monsieur, as an editor, will have observed that
a woman who is incapable in the daily affairs of life,
may reveal astounding force in an emergency? It
was so in this case. Madame put her foot down.
She showed unsuspected commercial aptitude. She
firmly forbade Dupont to do anything of the sort!

" 'What?' she exclaimed. 'You will telegraph to
her, inquiring? Never in this life! You might as
well advise her frankly not to come. What would
such a question mean? That you do not think the
place is good enough for her! Well, if *you* do not
think so, neither will *she*—she will decide that she
had a foolish impulse, and stay away!'

" 'Mon Dieu! do you dream that a woman accustomed to the Café de Paris, or Maxim's, would
choose to sup in an obscure little restaurant like
ours?' said Dupont, fuming. 'Do you dream that

I am going to buy partridges, and peaches, and
wines, and heaven knows what other delicacies, in
the dark? Do you dream that I am going to ruin
myself while every instinct in me protests? It would
be the act of a madman!'

" 'My little cabbage,' returned Madame, 'we are
so near to ruin as we are, that a step nearer is of
small importance. If Little-Flower-of-the-Wood
should come, it might be the turning-point in our
fortunes—people would hear of it, the Loup Blanc
might become renowned. Yes, we shall buy partridges, and peaches—also bonbons, and flowers, and
we shall hire a piano! And if the good fairies
should indeed send her to us, I swear she shall pass
as pleasant an evening as if she had gone to Voisin's,
or Paillard's itself!'

"Good! She convinced him. For the rest of the
day the Loup Blanc was in a state of frenzy. Never
before had such a repast been seen in its kitchen,
never before had he cooked with such loving care,
even when he had been preparing a dinner of ceremony on the Boulevard Haussmann. Madame herself ran out to arrange for the piano. The floor
was swept. The waiter was put into a clean shirt.
Dupont shed tears of excitement in his saucepans.

"He served the two-franc dinner that evening with
eyes that watched nothing but the clock. All his
consciousness now was absorbed by the question
whether the dancer would come or not. The dinner

passed somehow—it is to be assumed that the customers grumbled, but in his suspense Dupont regarded them with indifference. The hours crept by.
It was a quarter to twelve—twelve o'clock. He
trembled behind the counter as if with ague. Now
it was time that she was here! His face was
blanched, his teeth chattered in his head. What if
he had been hoaxed after all? Half-past twelve!
The sweat ran down him. Terror gripped his heart.
A vision of all the partridges wasted convulsed his
soul. Hark! a carriage stopped. He tottered forward. The door opened—she had come!

"Women are strange. Little-Flower-of-the-Wood,
who yawned her pretty head off at Armenonville,
was enraptured with the Loup Blanc. The rest of
the party took their tone from her, and everything
was pronounced 'fun,' the coarse linen, the dirty
ceiling, the admiring stares of the bock drinkers.
The lady herself declared that she had 'never enjoyed a supper so much in her life,' and the waiter—
it was not Adolphe then—was dumbfounded by a
louis tip.

"Figure yourself the exultation of Madame!
'Aha,' she chuckled, when they shut up shop at
sunrise, 'what did I tell you, my little cabbage?'
Monsieur, as an editor, will have observed that a
woman who reveals astounding force in an emergency may triumph pettily when the emergency is
over?

" 'It remains to be seen whether they will come any more, however,' said Dupont. 'Let us go to bed. Mon Dieu, how sleepy I am!' It was the first occasion that the Loup Blanc had been open till five in the morning.

"It was the first occasion, and for some days they feared it might be the last. But no, the dancer came again! A few eccentrics who came with her flattered themselves on having made a 'discovery.' They boasted of it. Gradually the name of 'Le Loup Blanc' became known. By the time that Little-Flower-of-the-Wood had had enough, there was a supper clientèle without her. Folly is infectious, and in Paris there are always people catching a fresh craze. Dupont began to put up his prices, and levied a charge on the waiter for the privilege of waiting at supper. The rest of the history is more grave! . . . Comment, Monsieur? Eh bien, if you insist, again an absinthe!"

Janiaud paused, and ran his dirty fingers through his hair.

"This man can talk!" said the Editor, in an undertone.

"Gentlemen," resumed the poet, "two years passed. Little-Flower-of-the-Wood was on the Italian Riviera. The Italian Riviera was awake again after the heat of the summer. The little town that had dozed for many months began to stir. Almost every day now she saw new faces on the promenade,

The sky was gentler, the sea was fairer. And she sat loathing it all, craving to escape from it to the bleak streets of Paris.

"Two winters before, she had been told, 'Your lungs will stand no more of the pranks you have been playing. You must go South, and keep early hours, or——' The shrug said the rest. And she had sold some of her diamonds and obeyed. Of course, it was an awful nuisance, but she must put up with it for a winter in order to get well. As soon as she was well, she would go back, and take another engagement! She had promised herself to be dancing again at the Ambassadeurs by May.

"But when May had come, she was no better. And travelling was expensive, and all places were alike to her since she was forbidden to return to Paris. She had disposed of more jewellery, and looked forward to the autumn. And in the autumn she had looked forward to the spring. So it had gone on.

"At first, while letters came to her sometimes, telling her how she was missed, the banishment had been alleviated; later, in her loneliness, it had grown frightful. Monsieur, her soul—that little soul that pleasure had held dumb—cried out, under misfortune, like a homeless child for its mother. Her longing took her by the throat, and the doctor had difficulty in dissuading her from going to meet death by the first train. She did not suspect that she was

doomed in any case; he thought it kinder to deceive her. He had preached 'Patience, mademoiselle, a little patience!' And she had wrung her
hands, but yielded—sustained by the hope of a future that she was never to know.

"By this time the last of her jewels was sold, and
most of the money had been spent. The fact
alarmed her when she dwelt upon it, but she did not
dwell upon it very often—in the career of Little-
Flower-of-the-Wood, so many pecuniary crises had
been righted at the last moment. No, although
there was nobody now to whom she could turn for
help, it was not anxiety that bowed her; the thoughts
by which she was stricken, as she sauntered feebly
on the eternal promenade, was that in Paris they
no longer talked of her, and that her prettiness had
passed away. She was forgotten, ugly! The tragedy of her exile was that.

"Now it was that she found out the truth—she
learnt that there was no chance of her recovering.
She made no reproaches for the lies that had been
told her; she recognised that they had been well
meant. All she said was, 'I am glad that it is not
too late; I may see Paris still before the curtain
tumbles—I shall go at once.'

"Not many months of life remained to her, but
they were more numerous than her louis. It was an
unfamiliar Paris that she returned to! She had
quitted the Paris of the frivolous and fêted; she

came back to the Paris of the outcast poor. The world that she had remembered gave her no welcome—she peered through its shut windows, friendless in the streets.

"Gentlemen, last night all the customers had gone from the little Restaurant au Loup Blanc but a woman in a shabby opera-cloak—a woman with tragic eyes, and half a lung. She sat fingering her glass of beer absently, though the clock over the desk pointed to a quarter to midnight, and at midnight beer-drinkers are no longer desired in the Loup Blanc. But she was a stranger; it was concluded that she didn't know!

"Adolphe approached to enlighten her; 'Madame wishes to order supper?' he asked.

The stranger shook her head.

" 'Madame will have champagne?'

" 'Don't bother me!' said the woman.

"Adolphe nodded towards the bock contemptuously. 'After midnight, only champagne is served here,' he said; 'it is the rule of the house.'

" 'A fig for the rule!' scoffed the woman; 'I am going to stop!'

"Adolphe retired and sought the 'patron,' and Dupont advanced to her with dignity.

" 'Madame is plainly ignorant of our arrangements,' he began; 'at twelve o'clock one cannot remain for the cost of a bock—the restaurant becomes very gay.'

" 'So I believe,' she said; 'I want to see the gaiety.'

" 'It also becomes expensive. I will explain! During the evening we serve a dinner at two francs for our customers in the neighbourhood—and until twelve o'clock one may order bocks, or what one wishes, at strictly moderate prices. But at twelve o'clock there is a change; we have quite a different class of trade. People who amuse themselves arrive here to sup and to dance. As a supper-house, the Loup Blanc is known to all Paris.'

" 'One lives and learns!' said the woman, ironically; 'but I know more about the Loup Blanc than you seem to think. I can tell you the history of its success.'

" 'Madame?' Dupont regarded her with haughty eyes.

" 'Three years ago, monsieur, the Loup Blanc stood where it stands now, but there was no "different class of trade" at twelve o'clock, and no champagne. The dinners at two francs for your customers in the neighbourhood were all that you aspired to! You did the cooking yourself in those days, and you did not sport a white waistcoat and a gold watch-chain.'

" 'These things have nothing to do with it. You will comply with the rule, or you must go. All is said!'

" 'One night Little-Flower-of-the-Wood had a whim to sup here,' continued the woman, as if he had not spoken. 'She had passed the place in her carriage and fancied its flag, or its flower-pot—or she wanted to do something new. Anyhow, she had the whim! I see you have the telephone behind the desk now, monsieur—your little restaurant was not on the telephone when she wished to reserve a table that night; she had to reserve it by a messenger.'

" 'Well, well?' said Dupont, impatiently.

" 'But you were a shrewd man, you saw your luck and leapt at it—and when she entered with her party, you received her like a queen! You had even hired a piano, you said, in case Little-Flower-of-the-Wood might wish to play. I notice that a piano is in the corner still—no doubt you soon saved the money to buy one.'

" 'How do you know all this, you?' Dupont's gaze was curious.

" 'Her freak pleased her, and she came again and again—and others came, just to see her here. Then you recognised that your customers from the neighbourhood were out of place among the spend-thrifts, who yielded more profit in a night than all the two-franc dinners in a month; you said, "At twelve o'clock there shall be no more bocks, only champagne!" I had made your restaurant famous —and you introduced the great rule that you now command me to obey!'

" 'You? You are Little-Flower-of-the-Wood?'

" 'Yes, it was I who did it for you,' she said

quietly. 'And the restaurant flourished after Little-Flower-of-the-Wood had faded. Well, to-night I want to spend an hour here again, for the sake of what I used to be. Time brings changes, you understand, and I cannot conform with the great rule.' She opened the opera cloak, trembling, and he saw that beneath it Little-Flower-of-the-Wood was in rags.

" 'I am very poor and ill,' she went on. 'I have been away in the South for more than two years; they told me I ought to stop there, but I had to see Paris once more! What does it matter? I shall finish here a little sooner, that is all. I lodge close by, in a garret. The garret is very dirty, but I hear the music from the Bal Tabarin across the way. I like that—I persuade myself I am living the happy life I used to have. When I am tossing sleepless, I hear the noise and laughter of the crowd coming out, and blow kisses to them in the dark. You see, although one is forgotten, one cannot forget. I pray that their laughter will come up to me right at the end, before I die!'

" 'You cannot afford to enter Tabarin's?' faltered Dupont; 'you are so stony as that?'

" 'So stony as that!' she said. 'And I repeat that to-night I want to pass an hour in the midst of the life I loved. Monsieur, remember how you came to make your rule! Break it for me once! Let me stay here to-night for a bock!'

"Dupont is a restaurateur, but he is also a man. He took both her hands, and the waiters were astonished to perceive that the 'patron' was crying.

" 'My child,' he stammered, 'you will sup here as my guest.'

"Adolphe set before her champagne that she sipped feverishly, and a supper that she was too ill to eat. And cabs came rattling from the Grands Boulevards with boisterous men and women who no longer recalled her name—and with other 'Little-Flowers-of-the-Wood,' who had sprung up since her day.

"The woman who used to reign there sat among them, looking back, until the last jest was bandied, and the last bottle was drained. Then she bade her host 'good-bye,' and crawled home—to the garret where she 'heard the music of the ball'; the garret where she 'prayed that the laughter would come up to her right at the end, before she died'! "

Janiaud finished the absinthe, and lurched to his feet. "That's all."

"Great Scott," said the Editor, "if he could only write in English! But——but it's very pitiable, she may starve there; something ought to be done. . . . Can you tell us where she is living, monsieur?"

The poet shrugged his shoulders. "Is there no satisfying you? You asked me for the history of the Loup Blanc; and there are things that even I do not know; however, I have done my best! I cannot say where the lady is living, but I can tell you where she was born." He pointed, with a drunken laugh, to his glass: "There!"

IV

DEAD VIOLETS

"IF you ever want me, write to me—I'd come to you from the end of the world!" he had said; and she had answered, "I shall always want you, but I shall never write, and you must never come." She was married.

It was in May that they parted; they parted on the day of her owning that she cared for him. The virtue was hers, not his; yet because he loved her, and realised that she was too good a woman to defy her conscience and be happy, he acquiesced in her decision—refrained from pleading to her, refrained from trying to see her again.

His only indulgence was to send violets to her home in Paris for the ninth of December; the ninth of December was her birthday, and violets, she had once told him, were her favourite flower. He did not scribble any greeting with them, did not even enclose a card; he was sure that she would know who sent them, and it lightened his pain to feel that she would know. Indeed, to recall himself to her thus mutely was a joy, the only joy that he had ex-

perienced since the day of the "good-bye"; almost
it was as if he were going to her, that moment in the
London florist's when he held the flowers that would
reach her hands; she did not seem so lost to him for
the moment, the separation did not seem so blank.

The next year, also, he sent violets for the ninth
of December. His emotions, it is true, were less
vivid this time, but he was glad to show her that he
was faithful; besides, the prettiness of the reminder
pleased him.

And the third year he sent them chiefly because
he felt that she would be disappointed if he appeared
to forget.

So it had grown to be his custom to send violets
to her for her birthday, though what was once an
impulse of devotion was now a falsehood—the
weakness of a sentimentalist reluctant to wound a
woman, and his self-esteem, by admitting that he had
exaggerated the importance of his feelings. And
each December the woman welcomed the lie with
smiles and tears, and believed that he loved her still.

When five years had passed he met her again. It
was in Bond Street, and he had sent the violets to
Paris two or three days before.

"Phil!"

As he turned and saw her, he thought how much
better-looking she used to be. (She was young still,
no more than thirty, but she had longed for him on
every day of the five years, and her tears had

blotted some of the girlishness from her face.) As he turned and saw her, the woman thought how his mouth had twitched when he said, "I'd come to you from the end of the world." It is among the un-acknowledged truths that sentimentality may create as much ferment as enduring love, and he had suf-fered even more violently than she, though he had not suffered so long.

"What are you doing here in December—you're the last person I should have expected to see?" she said.

"I go South to-morrow."

"Lucky man!"

"And you?"

"We're living here now."

"Really? You've left Paris? How long?"

"We've been here since October; we're flat-hunting."

"Oh!"

They stood looking into each other's eyes, neither knowing what to say next. Her heart was thumping terribly, and she felt very happy and very frightened. More than once she had been tempted to write to him that her courage had broken down; all resist-ance seemed to have left her as she stood looking into his eyes again.

"Flats," she added in a voice of composure, "are so abominably dear in London."

"Where are you staying?"

"In apartments—Bayswater."

"Bayswater must be a change from Neuilly? It was a jolly little place you had in Neuilly!"

"It was rather jolly, wasn't it? My—my husband's people wished us to come over; they thought they might put him into something over here. Of course, in Paris it was cheap, but there were no prospects."

"I understand."

"There's some talk of a secretaryship if a company is floated." It was so natural to be telling him everything now they had met. "It would be a very good thing for us."

"I hope it'll come off."

"Yes. . . . Well, how are you? I'm always seeing your name—'one of the novels of the year'!"

"They aren't so good as the novels that nobody reads."

"Not quite. Why?"

"I'm turning out what's wanted now. One has to live."

"Yes. . . . Still, isn't it a pity to—to——"

"Oh, one gets tired!" he said. "Ideals make lonely dwelling places. . . . Let me take you somewhere and give you some tea."

"I ought to go to some shops; I'm up West to work."

" 'Work'? Spending money?"

"Earning it—I'm doing fashion articles."

"You? Do you mean it? Well, come and have some tea first."

It was very early, and there were vacant tables in the alcoves. As he sat opposite her, Orlebar thought what a fraud it was that the things one craved for only came to pass when one had grown resigned to doing without them. How he had besought God for some such chance as this—what a spectacle he had made of himself about her during six unforgettable months! And now he was sipping tea without emotion, and observing that her clothes compared unfavourably with the other women's in the room! In that moment Orlebar saw the humiliating truth—knew that he had lived his great love down and deceived himself for years. But he didn't want to see—he preferred to deceive himself now. It is often more congenial to be an ass than to acknowledge that you have been one.

"It's a long time since we had tea together, Lucy!"

"Yes," she said.

"Well, what have you got to tell me?"

"I think I told you everything in a breath; at least—— What have you been doing all the time?"

"Trying to kill it."

"You're working in London now, eh?"

"Yes. I've chambers in the Temple. Rather swagger compared with the little shanty in the Rue Ravignan! How did you come to take up journalism?"

"Someone suggested it—and my twaddle seemed to do. It's pretty sickening."

"What's the idea—it doesn't pay very well, does it?"

"Not on my paper; I get a guinea a week, but—— Oh, why should I bore you with all that?"

"You don't 'bore' me, Lucy."

"Well, I—I prefer to do it! You don't know everything; his people have never forgiven his marriage—they think marriage has handicapped him so badly—and, you may be sure, they blame me more than him; it's always the daughter-in-law's fault! We've only their allowance to live on—it isn't pleasant to be kept by people who resent your existence!"

"Poor little woman! No, I didn't know."

"Oh, it's not so bad as all that! Still, I'm glad to be making something, even if it's only a guinea a week. I don't feel so uncomfortable when I meet them, not such a dead weight. We have to go there to dinner on Sundays, and it's rather awful—they tell me what a splendid career he would have had if he hadn't married!"

"Damn 'em!" said Orlebar.

"I do—every Sunday afternoon, from the soup to the coffee! Well"—she leant her elbows on the table, and smiled—"have I changed much?"

"No," he said, bravely. "But—but this is brutal hard lines—I didn't dream that you had things like that to put up with! You always seemed so light-hearted in Paris."

"I didn't meet his people in Paris! Besides, things alter in five years; I think—— Oh!" she broke off, "it's ridiculous to talk about it to you, I don't know why I'm doing it!"

"Have you anybody else to talk to?"

"No," she admitted, slowly, "that's it! I can't talk to *him* because——well, they're his own people, for one thing; and, besides——well, of course, marriage *has* handicapped him, and I suppose he knows it as well as they do."

"Do you mean——? . . . You don't get on now?"

She gave a shrug, and traced lines on the cloth with her spoon; "What do you suppose I mean?"

"I am so sorry for you, dear!"

"Oh, I daresay it's my fault! I suppose I don't do all I ought to make up for what I've cost him; it's difficult to do all you ought when——when——" her voice snapped—"when you sometimes wish to God that you hadn't done so much!"

"Perhaps you'd have done better to come to me, after all," said Orlebar heavily; he couldn't think of anything else to say.

"I tried to be a good woman—I thought you'd forget me; *I* wanted to forget *you!* Why didn't you let me forget you? Why did you send me those flowers every year?"

"Were you vexed with me for sending them?"

"No."

"I'm glad.   I sent some to Paris the other day."

"Did you?   I wondered if you would; I've been
rather impatient for my birthdays.   What a confession—a woman impatient for her birthdays! I never
meant to see you any more, though; I swore I
wouldn't!"

"But you wanted to, didn't you?"

Her cup was neglected now; she leant back in the
chair, her hands clenched in her lap.

"Didn't you?" he repeated.

"Oh, don't!" she said in her throat.   "I can't
bear it, Phil!"

"What?"

"The life—everything\.   I'm tired of it all."

"Chuck it!" he muttered; "come away with me
to-morrow!"

She didn't speak; she tried to believe that she was
struggling.   The pause seemed to Orlebar to last a
long time while he sat wishing that he hadn't said it.
The waitress inquired if they required anything else,
and put the check on the table, and took her tip.
The place was filling, and a ladies' orchestra began
to twang their mandolines.

"Do you want me?" she asked, raising her eyes.

"Do I 'want' you!"   What else could he reply?

"Very well, then."   She nodded.   "I'll go! . . .

Let's get out of this—do you mind?—my head aches."

He knew dismally that her consent had come too late, that there would be nothing now to compensate him for the scandal—no months, or weeks, or even minutes of rapture. They got up, and he put the half-crown on the desk, and followed her into the street.

After they had strolled a few yards in silence, he said, as it seemed obligatory, "You've made me very happy!"

She answered, "I'll try to!" He wished that she had said anything else—it was painful.

"We'd better have a cab. Where shall we go—will you come to the Temple?"

"I think I'd like to go home; you can drive there with me."

"Can you get away in the morning—or shall I put it off?" he asked in the hansom.

"No, I can get away—he won't be back till the evening."

"Back from where?"

"He went down to his people to-day—they're in Brighton now. What time's the train?"

"Ten o'clock—from Charing Cross; I was going by Folkestone and Boulogne. Are you a bad sailor?"

"No, I like it. We'll meet at Charing Cross, then?"

"Yes; in the first-class waiting-room—if you're sure it's not too early for you?"

"It's all right. . . . Is it real, Phil? Half an hour ago we hadn't seen each other; and now—it's to be all our lives! Oh, I hope you'll never be sorry! I wonder?"

"That's unjust."

"Is it?" Her eyes reminded him that he ought to kiss her, and he bent his head. . . . He pitied her acutely as he felt her tears on his face—hated himself for lying to her.

"Cheer up, dearest! Remember how we care for each other," he said.

The effort of affecting joy wore him out as they drove on; intensely he wished that they had found a quicker cab; he wanted a drink badly, wanted to light a pipe and give way to his gloom. Her hand, which he clasped, seemed to him to grow larger and heavier through the long drive; and when at last they parted at her door, he thanked heaven for the right to heave a sigh, for the freedom to look as moody as he felt.

Five years ago! If it had only happened five—four years ago! The pathos of the situation took him by the throat. What a rotten thing life was! Again his mind reverted to the months when he had been torn with longing for her—the longing just to watch her, to listen to her, no matter what she said. And now he had kissed her for the first time—as a duty! The abandonment of despair had played havoc with him, yet he wished that it had lasted—it would have been worth while, he thought. God! the ecstasy that would have been thrilling in him now if he had suffered like that until this afternoon!

At the club he ordered a "big whisky and a small soda."

"You're off to Rome soon, aren't you?" said a man presently. "You pampered novelists have all the luck!"

"Yes," said Orlebar. The man was the Editor of a daily paper; it occurred to the novelist that he was about to provide the paper with some surprising "copy"; also that the editorial greeting would be less informal when they met again.

What a deuce of a lot of talk there would be! the damage it was going to do him socially! Socially? It would injure him financially, too; he recognised it for the first time as he surveyed the room. There was McKinnell, of the *Mayfair,* ragging a waiter because the toast was cold; Orlebar's new novel was to run through the *Mayfair* before it came out in book form. If he knew anything of McKinnell, that highly respectable gentleman would refuse to pollute the pages of his journal with the fiction of a co-respondent. And McKinnell's refusal wouldn't be singular, though he might express it with singular offensiveness. Even among good fellows, it would be, "Sorry, but we daren't run you just now in a

paper for household reading—we should get no end
of protests. Awful rot, of course, but there it is!"
Five hundred pounds gone! Five hundred pounds
was a large sum; he was no millionaire.

And his books? The sale of his next books would
drop in this virtuous country when he had outraged
the Eleventh Commandment. If she had been
"Lady" somebody the public would have called the
case "romantic"—it would have been a big advertisement then—but without the glamour of a title
they would only call it "disgraceful." For one
reader gained by the scandal, half a dozen would be
lost. What a calamity, his turning into Bond Street
this afternoon!

And how she had jumped at him, he thought with
sudden resentment; she hadn't needed much persuasion! He had been an idiot to exalt her into a
heroine at the beginning—since it had been fated
that he was to ruin himself, he might at any rate
have done it while he was in love with her! And he
hadn't even the excuse of youth now; he was making
a mess of his life when he was old enough to know
better—he was ruining himself against his will! He
had another whisky-and-soda, and wondered if there
was any chance of his hearing that she had changed
her mind. Confound it, she didn't know his address!
And anyhow there would be no chance; what was
she giving up—a husband who didn't want her. If
she had had a child, it would have been a different

thing. A pity she hadn't a family! "A husband who didn't want her." And he, Philip Orlebar, was going to take her off his hands! Oh, what a mug's game! If he hadn't gone in to have his hat ironed, he wouldn't have met her. And it hadn't really needed ironing either!

He did not remain long in the club when dinner was over. After all, he had mentioned that his rooms were in the Temple, and the hope that she might try to communicate with him lingered in spite of common-sense. At the gate he looked towards the porter eagerly, but the porter said nothing, and the shock of disappointment told Orlebar how strong the hope had been.

His portmanteaux were half-packed, and he spent the evening straining to catch the sound of the bell. Once it rang, but the visitor was only a bore who had dropped in for a drink and a chat. Orlebar loathed the beaming face as he gave him welcome, and, like the Editor, the bore made envious reference to the morrow's journey; he "wished he were in the author's shoes!" Orlebar was at infinite pains to affect high spirits, for it was undesirable that the man should say afterwards, "I was with him the night before he bolted with her—the poor beggar seemed to have an awful hump." But presently the man said, "You seem a cup low to-night, old chap?" The melancholy stroke of the Temple clock had never sounded so lugubrious as in the hours that followed.

When he woke in the morning, Orlebar remembered that there ought to be a half-bottle of Pommery in the bathroom, and he had it in lieu of tea, with some biscuits. The wine lightened his mood a little; it no longer seemed so hopelessly impossible to conceal his regret; and when he strode into the station, it was with a very fair show of impatience. But his heart leapt as he saw that she wasn't there. He sat on a couch, glanced alternately at the clock and the doors, and praying that she wouldn't come.

She entered just as he was feeling sanguine.

"My darling!" he murmured, "here you are!"

"Am I late?"

"I was beginning to be afraid. But there's time enough—I've got the tickets. Where's your luggage?"

"They've taken it through."

"We'd better go, then."

Among the bustle on the platform he could say little more than, "How pale you are!" and "Which are your trunks?" Then they were alone, and the door had been slammed, and the train moved out.

"Darling!" he said again. "Well?"

"Well?"

"It seems too good to be true." His tone was lifeless.

"Does it!"

"Doesn't it to you?"

"I think it's true," she said, with a tired smile.

"How pale you are!" he repeated. "Didn't you sleep?"

"Not much. I've been wondering."

" 'Wondering'? What?"

"Whether I ought to have said 'no.' What would you have done if I'd said 'no,' Phil? Really?"

"What *can* a man do? I suppose I should have had to put up with it."

She didn't reply for a moment. She was gazing straight before her, with a frown.

"Do you think me a bad woman, Phil?"

"I think you're the best woman I've ever known."

"It looks like it, doesn't it!"

"The force of circumstances! If you had met me before you met him——"

"But I didn't. It's pretty mean of me to spoil his life, isn't it?"

"I didn't know that he cared so much about you?"

"Oh"—she hesitated—"we've quarrelled, like everybody else, but—but he's very fond of me. Of course, it'll be an awful blow. I can't forget it— I've been thinking of it ever since."

"It just depends . . . the thing you've got to consider is which way you'll be happier yourself. If—I don't know! I suppose there are women who *can't* go wrong and be happy!"

"I'm thinking of my duty," she faltered. "You know I love you, don't you? I want you to know it, to keep remembering it all the time. I love you, I love, I love you! But——" She waited with her heart in her throat.

"But what?" he asked, moodily. "What were you going to say?" Her eyes closed with the pain.

"Eh?" he said.

"There are his people," she stammered; "they'll feel the disgrace so much. I've been considering everything—I—I didn't know what a wrench it would be."

"You'll get over it."

"I'm not sure. Perhaps I shall always——? Do you think I've . . . made a mistake?" Again she waited breathlessly. If he would only seize her in his arms! If he would only cry, "Let them all go to the devil, and remember *me!*"

"If you feel like that," he said feebly, "of course I hardly—I hardly know what I can say to you."

"You can't *think* of anything to say?" she pleaded. "There's nothing—nothing I'm overlooking?"

"There's time; one gets over anything in time," he said incautiously.

"Oh, my God!" she moaned.

She turned to the window, her face as white as a dead woman's. The terror was confirmed that had stolen on her in the cab, that had haunted her throughout the night—confirmed by his tones, his looks, by every answer he had made to her halting falsehoods; he had learnt to do without her, she had given herself unsought! In the agony of shame that overwhelmed her she could have thrown herself from the compartment; and, mark this! it was only her love for him that restrained her—she would not reproach him by deed, or word, he shouldn't be burdened by the knowledge of what he had made her suffer.

"Well," he said, "it's not too late."

"No," she muttered, "I can't go!"

His pulses jumped; for an instant he couldn't trust his voice.

"You must do as you like, I don't want to take you against your will. . . . If you wish it, you can go back from Folkestone; I suppose—if he's away—there'd be no harm done, would there?"

"You're not angry with me? You won't mind too much!"

"Don't worry about *me*—I want *you* to be happy. To tell you the truth, I think you're right—you're not the woman to kick over the traces, you'd be too cut up about it. Go back and make the best of a bad business—it'll be easier for you to bear than the other, anyhow! We'll see about a train for you as soon as we get in."

At Folkestone Harbour they ascertained that there would be an express to Charing Cross at two o'clock, and he paced the platform with her till it was time to say "good-bye." Exhilaration had given him an appetite, but she answered that she wasn't hungry; so, as he had missed his boat, he decided to drive to an hotel on the Leas and have an elaborate luncheon when she had gone. His glances at the playbills on the walls showed him that *San Toy* was at the Pleasure Gardens, and he foresaw himself cheerfully among the audience in the evening. He was feeling on a sudden twenty years younger, and, hard as he strove to acquire a manner of tender gravity, she discerned the improvement in his spirits every time he spoke.

Her train arrived in town at a few minutes to four, and she re-entered the lodging-house some hours earlier than her husband. But the fire had gone out, and she had to wait shivering till it was lighted before she could burn the note that she had left on the mantelpiece for him. A little box addressed to her had been delivered during her absence; when the slatternly servant left her alone at last, the woman dared to touch it—and fell to sobbing as if her heart would burst. It contained the violets that Orlebar had sent in token of his love.

The box had been redirected from Paris. Owing to the delay, the violets, now that they reached her, were quite dead.

V

THE DANGER OF BEING A TWIN

My Confession must begin when I was four years old and recovering from swollen glands. As I grew well, my twin-brother, Grégoire, who was some minutes younger, was put to bed with the same complaint.

"What a misfortune," exclaimed our mother, "that Silvestre is no sooner convalescent than Grégoire falls ill!"

The doctor answered: "It astonishes me that you were not prepared for it, Madame Lapalme—since the children are twins, the thing was to be foreseen; when the elder throws the malady off, the younger naturally contracts it. Among twins it is nearly always so."

And it always proved to be so with Grégoire and me. No sooner did I throw off whooping-cough than Grégoire began to whoop, though I was at home in Vernon and he was staying with our grandmother in Tours. If I had to be taken to a dentist, Grégoire would soon afterwards be howling with toothache; as often as I indulged in the pleasures of the table, Grégoire had a bilious attack. The influence I exercised upon him was so remarkable, that once when my bicycle ran away with me and broke my arm, our mother consulted three medical men as to whether Grégoire's bicycle was bound to run away with him too. Indeed, my brother was distinctly apprehensive of it himself.

Of course, the medical men explained that he was susceptible to any abnormal physical or mental condition of mine, not to the vagaries of my bicycle. "As an example, madame, if the elder of two twins were killed in a railway accident, it would be no reason for thinking that an accident must befall a train by which the younger travelled. What sympathy can there be between locomotives? But if the elder were to die by his own hand, there is a strong probability that the younger would commit suicide also."

However, I have not died by my own hand, so Grégoire has had nothing to reproach me for on that score. As to other grounds—well, there is much to be said on both sides!

To speak truly, that beautiful devotion for which twins are so celebrated in drama and romance has never existed between my brother and myself. Nor was this my fault. I was of a highly sensitive disposition, and from my earliest years it was impressed upon me that Grégoire regarded me in the light of a grievance. I could not help having illnesses, yet he would upbraid me for taking them. Then, too, he was always our mother's favourite, and instead of there being caresses and condolence for me when I was indisposed, there was nothing but grief for the indisposition that I was about to cause Grégoire. This wounded me.

Again at college. I shall not pretend that I was a bookworm, or that I shared Grégoire's ambitions; on the contrary, the world beyond the walls looked such a jolly place to me that the mere sight of a classroom would sometimes fill me with abhorrence. But, mon Dieu! if other fellows were wild occasionally, they accepted the penalties, and the affair was finished; on me rested a responsibility—my wildness was communicated to Grégoire. Scarcely had I resigned myself to dull routine again than Grégoire, the industrious, would find himself unable to study a page, and would commit freaks for which he rebuked me most sternly. I swear that my chief remembrance of my college days is Grégoire addressing pompous homilies to me in this fashion, when he was in disgrace with the authorities:—

"I ask you to remember, Silvestre, that you have not only your own welfare to consider—you have mine! I am here to qualify myself for an earnest career. Be good enough not to put obstacles in my path. Your levity impels me to distractions which I condemn even while I yield to them. I perceive a weakness in your nature that fills me with misgivings

for my future; if you do not learn to resist temptation, to what errors may I not be driven later on—
to what outbreaks of frivolity will you not condemn
me when we are men?"

Well, it is no part of my confession to whitewash myself—his misgivings were realised! So far
as I had any serious aspirations at all, I aspired to
be a painter, and, after combating my family's objections, I entered an art-school in Paris. Grégoire,
on the other hand, was destined for the law. During the next few years we met infrequently, but that
my brother continued to be affected by any unusual
conditions of my body and mind I knew by his letters, which seldom failed to contain expostulations
and entreaties. If he could have had his way,
indeed, I believe he would have shut me in a
monastery.

Upon my word, I was not without consideration
for him, but what would you have? To me, also,
I think some sympathy was due. Regard the situation with my eyes! I was young, popular, an
artist; my life was no more frivolous than the lives
of others of my set; yet, in lieu of being free, like
them, to call the tune and dance the measure, I was
burdened with a heavier responsibility than weighs
upon the shoulders of any paterfamilias. Let me
but drink a bottle too much, and Grégoire, the
grave, would subsequently manifest all the symptoms
of intoxication. Let me but lose my head about a

petticoat, and Grégoire, the righteous, would soon
be running after a girl instead of attending to his
work. I had a conscience—thoughts of the trouble
that I was brewing for Grégoire would come between me and the petticoat and rob it of its charms.
His abominable susceptibility to my caprices marred
half my pleasures for me. Once when I sat distrait,
bowed by such reflections, a woman exclaimed,
"What's the matter with you! One would think
you had a family!" "Well," I said, "I have a
twin!" And I went away. She was a pretty woman,
too!

Do you suppose that Maître Lapalme—he was
Maître Lapalme by then, this egregious Grégoire—
do you suppose that he wrote to bless me for my
sacrifice? Not at all! Of my heroisms he knew
nothing—he was only conscious of my lapses. To
read his letters one would have imagined that I was
a reprobate, a creature without honour or remorse.
I quote from one of them—it is a specimen of them
all. Can you blame me if I had no love for this
correspondent?

MY BROTHER,

THE CIRCUMSTANCES OF OUR BIRTH:—

Your attention is directed to my preceding communications on
this subject. I desire to protest against the revelry from which
you recovered either on the 15th or 16th inst. On the afternoon
of the latter date, while engaged in a conference of the first
magnitude, I was seized with an overwhelming desire to dance a

quadrille at a public ball. I found it impossible to concentrate
my attention on the case concerning which I was consulted; I
could no longer express myself with lucidity. Outwardly sedate,
reliable, I sat at my desk dizzied by such visions as pursued St.
Anthony to his cell. No sooner was I free than I fled from
Vernon, dined in Paris, bought a false beard, and plunged wildly
into the vortex of a dancing-hall. Scoundrel! This is past
pardon! My sensibilities revolt, and my prudence shudders.
Who shall say but that one night I may be recognized? Who
can foretell to what blackmail you may expose me? I, Maitre
Lapalme, forbid your profligacies, which devolve upon me; I
forbid,——" etc.

Such admissions my brother sent to me in a dis-
guised handwriting, and unsigned; perhaps, he
feared that his blackmailer might prove to be
myself!

Our mother still lived in Vernon, where she contemplated her favourite son's success with the pro-
foundest pride. Occasionally I spent a few days
with her, sometimes even more, for she always
pressed me to remain. I think she pressed me to
remain, not from any pleasure in my society, but
because she knew that while I was at home I could
commit no actions that would corrupt Grégoire. One
summer, when I visited her, I met Mademoiselle
Leuillet.

Mademoiselle Leuillet was the daughter of a
widower, a neighbour. I remember that when our
servant first announced her, I thought, "What a
nuisance; how bored I am going to be!" And then
she came in, and in an instant I was spellbound.

I am tempted to describe Berthe Leuillet to you as she entered our salon that afternoon in a white frock, with a basket of roses in her little hands, but I know very well that no description of a girl ever painted her to anybody yet. Suffice it that she was as beautiful as an angel, that her voice was like the music of the Spheres—more than all, that one felt all the time, "How good she is, how good, how good!"

I suppose the impression that she made upon me was plainly to be seen, for when she had gone, my mother remarked, "You did not say much; are you always so silent in girls' company?" "No," I answered, "I do not often meet such girls."

But afterwards I often met Berthe Leuillet.

Never since I was a boy had I stayed in Vernon for so long as now; never had I repented so bitterly as now the error of my ways. I loved, and it seemed to me sometimes that my attachment was reciprocated, yet my position forbade me to go to Monsieur Leuillet and ask boldly for his daughter's hand. While I had remained obscure, artists of my acquaintance, whose talent was no more remarkable than my own, had raised themselves from bohemia into prosperity. I abused myself, I acknowledged that I was an idler, a good-for-nothing, I declared that the punishment that had overtaken me was no more than I deserved. And then—well, then I owned to Berthe that I loved her!

Deliberately I should not have done this before seeking her father's permission, but it happened in the hour of our "good-bye," and I was suffering too deeply to subdue the impulse. I owned that I loved her—and when I left for Paris we were secretly engaged.

Mon Dieu! Now I worked indeed! To win this girl for my own, to show myself worthy of her innocent faith, supplied me with the most powerful incentive in life. In the Quartier they regarded me first with ridicule, then with wonder, and, finally, with respect. For my enthusiasm did not fade. "He has turned over a new leaf," they said, "he means to be famous!" It was understood. No more excursions for Silvestre, no more junketings and recklessness! In the morning as soon as the sky was light I was at my easel; in the evening I studied, I sketched, I wrote to Berthe, and re-read her letters. I was another man—my ideal of happiness was now a wife and a home.

For a year I lived this new life. I progressed. Men—men whose approval was a cachet—began to speak of me as one with a future. In the Salon a picture of mine made something of a stir. How I rejoiced, how grateful and sanguine I was! All Paris sang "Berthe" to me; the criticisms in the papers, the felicitations of my friends, the praise of the Public, all meant Berthe—Berthe with her arms about me, Berthe on my breast!

I said that it was not too soon for me to speak now; I had proved my mettle, and, though I foresaw that her father would ask more before he gave his consent, I was, at least, justified in avowing myself. I telegraphed to my mother to expect me; I packed my portmanteau with trembling hands, and threw myself into a cab.

On the way to the station, I noticed the window of a florist's; I bade the driver stop, and ran in to bear off some lilies for Berthe. The shop was so full of wonderful flowers that, once among them, I found some difficulty in making my choice. Hence I missed the train, and returned to my studio, incensed by the delay. A letter for me had just been delivered. It told me that on the previous morning Berthe had married my brother.

I could have welcomed a pistol shot—my world rocked. Berthe lost, false, Grégoire's wife! I reiterated it, I said it over and over, I was stricken by it—and yet I could not realise that actually it had happened. It seemed too treacherous, too horrible to be true.

Oh, I made certain of it later, believe me—I was no hero of a feuilleton, to accept such intelligence without proof! I assured myself of her perfidy, and burnt her love letters one by one; tore her photographs into shreds—strove also to tear her image from my heart.

Ah, that mocked me, that I could not tear! A

year before I should have rushed to the cafés for forgetfulness, but now, as the shock subsided, I turned feverishly to work. I told myself that she had wrecked my peace, my faith in women, that I hated and despised her; but I swore that she should not have the triumph of wrecking my career, too. I said that my art still remained to me—that I would find oblivion in my art.

Brave words! But one does not recover from such blows so easily.

For months I persisted, denying myself the smallest respite, clinging to a resolution which proved vainer daily. Were art to be mastered by dogged endeavour, I should have conquered, but alas! though I could compel myself to paint, I could not compel myself to paint well. It was the perception of this fact that shattered me at last. I had fought temptation for half a year, worked with my teeth clenched, worked against nature, worked while my pulses beat and clamoured for the draughts of dissipation, which promised a speedier release. I had woed Art, not as her lover, but as a tortured soul may turn to one woman in the desperate hope of subduing his passion for another—and Art would yield nothing to a suitor who approached her so; I recognised that my work had been wasted, that the struggle had been useless—I broke down.

I need say little of the months that followed—it would be a record of degradations, and remorse;

alternately, I fell, and was ashamed. There were days when I never left the house, when I was repulsive to myself! I shuddered at the horrors that I had committed. No saint has loved virtue better than I did during those long sick days of self-disgust; no man was ever more sure of defying such hideous temptations if they recurred. As my lassitude passed I would take up my brushes and feel confident for an hour, or for a week. And then temptation would creep on me once more—humming in my ears, and tingling in my veins. And temptation had lost its loathsomeness now—it looked again attractive. It was a siren, it dizzied my conscience, and stupefied my common-sense. Back to the mire!

One afternoon when I returned to my rooms, from which I had been absent since the previous day, I heard from the concierge that a visitor awaited me. I climbed the stairs without anticipation. My thoughts were sluggish, my limbs leaden, my eyes heavy and bloodshot. Twilight had gathered, and as I entered I discerned merely the figure of a woman. Then she advanced—and all Hell seemed to leap flaring to my heart. My visitor was Berthe.

I think nearly a minute must have passed while we looked speechlessly in each other's face—hers convulsed by entreaty, mine dark with hate.

"Have you no word for me?" she whispered.

"Permit me to offer my congratulations on your

marriage, madame," I said. "I have had no earlier opportunity."

"Forgive me," she gasped, "I have come to beseech your forgiveness! Can you not forget the wrong I did you?"

"Do I look as if I had forgotten?"

"I was inconstant, cruel, I cannot excuse myself. But, O Silvestre, in the name of the love you once bore me, have pity on us! Reform, abjure your evil courses! Do not, I implore you, condemn my husband to this abyss of depravity; do not wreck my married life!"

Now I understood what had procured me the honour of a visit from this woman, and I triumphed devilishly that I was the elder twin.

"Madame," I answered, "I think that I owe you no explanations, but I shall say this: the evil courses that you deplore were adopted, not vindictively, but in the effort to numb the agony that you had made me suffer. You but reap as you have sown."

"Reform!" she sobbed. She sank on her knees before me. "Silvestre, in mercy to us, reform!"

"I will never reform," I said inflexibly. "I will grow more abandoned day by day—my past faults shall shine as merits compared with the atrocities that are to come. False girl, monster of selfishness, you are dragging me to the gutter, and your only grief is that *he* must share my shame! You have robbed me of my soul, and you have no regret but that my iniquities must re-act on *him!* By the shock that stunned him in the first flush of your honeymoon, you know what I experienced when I received the news of your deceit; by the anguish of repentance that overtakes him after each of his orgies, which revolt you, you know that I was capable of being a nobler man. The degradation that you behold is your own work. You have made me bad, and you must bear the consequences—you cannot now make me good to save your husband!"

Humbled and despairing, she left me.

I repeat that it is no part of my confession to palliate my guilt; the sight of her had served merely to inflame my resentment—and it was at this stage that I began deliberately to contemplate revenge.

But not the one that I had threatened. Oh, no! I bethought myself of a vengeance more complete than that! What, after all, were these escapades of his that were followed by contrition, that saw him again and again a penitent at her feet? There should be no more of such trifles; she should be tortured with the torture that she had dealt to me— I would make him adore another woman with all his heart and brain!

It was difficult, for first I must adore, and tire, of another woman myself—as my own passion faded, his would be born. I swore, however, that I would compass it, that I would worship some woman for a year—two years, as long as possible. Though he would be at peace in the meantime, the longer my enslavement lasted, the longer Berthe would suffer when her punishment began.

For some weeks now I worked again, to provide myself with money. I bought new clothes and made myself presentable. When my appearance accorded better with my plan, I paraded Paris, seeking the woman to adore.

You may think Paris is full of adorable women? Well, so contrary is human nature, that never had I felt such indifference towards the sex as during that tedious quest; never had a pair of brilliant eyes, or a well-turned neck appealed to me so little. After a month, my search seemed hopeless; I had viewed women by the thousand, but not one with whom I could persuade myself that I might fall violently in love.

How true it is that only the unforeseen comes to pass! There was a model, one Louise, whose fortune was her back, and who had long bored me by an evident tenderness. One day, this Louise, usually so constrained in my presence, appeared in high spirits, and mentioned that she was going to be married.

The change in her demeanour interested me; for the first time, I perceived that the attractions of Louise were not limited to her back. A little piqued, I invited her to dine with me. If she had said "yes," doubtless that would have been the end of my interest; but she refused. Before I parted from her, I made an appointment for her to sit to me the next morning.

"So you are going to be married, Louise?" I said carelessly, as I set the palette.

"In truth!" she answered.

"No regrets?"

"What regrets could I have? He is a very pretty boy, and well-to-do, believe me!"

"And *I* am not a pretty boy, nor well-to-do, hein?"

"Oh," she laughed, "you do not care for me!"

"Is it so?" I said. "What would you say if I told you that I did care?"

"I should say that you told me too late, monsieur," she replied, with a shrug. "Are you ready for me to pose?" And this changed woman turned her peerless back on me without a scruple.

A little mortified, I attended strictly to business for the rest of the morning. But I found myself, on the following day, waiting for her with impatience.

"And when is the event to take place?" I inquired, more eagerly than I chose to acknowledge. This was by no means the sort of enchantress that I had been seeking, you understand.

"In the spring," she said. "Look at the ring he has given to me, monsieur; is it not beautiful?"

I remarked that Louise's hands were very well

shaped, and, indeed, happiness had brought a certain charm to her face.

"Do you know, Louise, that I am sorry that you are going to marry?" I exclaimed.

"Oh, get out!" she laughed, pushing me away. "It is no good your talking nonsense to me now, don't flatter yourself!"

Pouchin, the sculptor, happened to come in at that moment. "Oho," he shouted, "what changes are to be seen! The nose of our brave Silvestre is out of joint now we are affianced, hein?"

She joined in his laughter against me, and I picked up my brush again in a vile humour.

Well, as I have said, she was not the kind of woman I had contemplated, but these things arrange themselves—I became seriously enamoured of her. And, recognising that Fate works with her own instruments, I did not struggle. For months I was at Louise's heels; I was the sport of her whims, and her slights, sometimes even of her insults. I actually made her an offer of marriage, at which she snapped her white fingers, with a grimace—and the more she flouted me, the more fascinated I grew. In that rapturous hour when her insolent eyes softened to sentiment, when her mocking mouth melted to a kiss, I was in Paradise. My ecstasy was so supreme that I forgot to triumph at my approaching vengeance.

So I married Louise; and yesterday was the

twentieth anniversary of our wedding. Berthe? To speak the truth, my plot against her was frustrated by an accident. You see, before I could communicate my passion to Grégoire I had to recover from it, and—this insolent Louise!—I have not recovered from it yet. There are days when she turns her remarkable back on me now—generally when I am idle—but, mon Dieu! the moments when she turns her lips are worth working for. Therefore, Berthe has been all the time quite happy with the good Grégoire—and since I possess Louise, upon my word of honour I do not mind!

VI

HERCULES AND APHRODITE

MADEMOISELLE CLAIRETTE used to say that if a danseuse could not throw a glance to the conductor of the band without the juggler being jealous, the Variety Profession was coming to a pretty pass. She also remarked that for a girl to entrust her life's happiness to a jealous suitor would be an act of lunacy. And then "Little Flouflou, the Juggling Genius," who was dying to marry her, would suffer tortures. He tried hard to conquer his failing, but it must be owned that Clairette's glances were very expressive, and that she distributed them indiscriminately. In Chartres, one night, he was so upset that he missed the umbrella, and the cigar, and the hat one after another, and instead of condoling with him when he came off the stage, all she said was "Butter-fingers!"

"Promise to be my wife," he would entreat: "it is not knowing where I am that gives me the pip. If you consented, I should be as right as rain—your word is as good to me as any Management's contract. I trust you; it is only myself that I doubt——

every time you look at a man I wonder, 'Am I up to
that chap's mark, is my "turn" as clever as his, isn't
it likely he will cut me out with her?' If you only
belonged to me I should never be jealous again as
long as I lived. Straight!"

And Clairette would answer firmly, "Poor boy,
you couldn't help it—you are made like that.
There'd be ructions every week, I should be for ever
in hot water. I like you very much, Flouflou, but
I'm not going to play the giddy goat. Chuck it!"

Nevertheless, he continued to worship her—from
her tawdry tiara to her tinselled shoes—and everybody was sure that it would be a match one day.
That is to say, everybody was sure of it until the
Strong Man had joined the troupe.

Hercule was advertised as "The Great Paris
Star." Holding himself very erect, he strutted, in
his latticed foot-gear, with stiff little steps, and in-
flated lungs, to the footlights, and tore chains to
pieces as easily as other people tear bills. He lay
down and supported a posse of mere mortals, and
a van-load of "properties" on his chest, and regained
his feet with a skip and a smirk. He—but his
achievements are well known. Preceding these feats
of force, was a feature of his entertainment which
Hercule enjoyed inordinately. He stood on a pedestal and struck attitudes to show the splendour of
his physique. Wearing only a girdle of tiger-skin,
and bathed in limelight, he felt himself to be as

glorious as a god.   The applause was a nightly intoxication to him.   He lived for it.   All day he looked forward to the moment when he could mount the pedestal again and make his biceps jump, and exhibit the magnificence of his highly developed back to hundreds of wondering eyes.   No woman was ever vainer of her form than was Hercule of his. No woman ever contemplated her charms more tenderly than Hercule regarded his muscles.   The latter half of his "turn" was fatiguing, but to posture in the limelight, while the audience stared open-mouthed and admired his nakedness, that was fine, it was dominion, it was bliss.

Hercule had never experienced a great passion— the passion of vanity excepted—never waited in the rain at a street corner for a coquette who did not come, nor sighed, like the juggler, under the window of a girl who flouted his declarations.   He had but accepted homage.   So when he fell in love with Clairette, he didn't know what to make of it.

For Clairette, sprightly as she was, did not encourage Hercule.   He at once attracted and repelled her.   When he rent chains, and poised prodigious weights above his head, she thrilled at his prowess, but the next time he attitudinised in the tiger-skin she turned up her nose.   She recognised something feminine in the giant.   Instinct told her that by disposition the Strong Man was less manly than

Little Flouflou, whom he could have swung like an Indian-club.

No, Hercule didn't know what to make of it. It was a new and painful thing to find himself the victim instead of the conqueror. For once in his career, he hung about the wings wistfully, seeking a sign of approval. For once he displayed his majestic figure on the pedestal blankly conscious of being viewed by a woman whom he failed to impress.

"What do you think of my turn?" he questioned at last.

"Oh, I have seen worse," was all she granted.

The giant winced.

"I am the strongest man in the world," he proclaimed.

"I have never met a Strong Man who wasn't!" said she.

"But there is someone stronger than I am," he owned humbly. (Hercule humble!) "Do you know what you have done to me, Clairette? You have made a fool of me, my dear."

"Don't be so cheeky," she returned. "Who gave you leave to call me 'my dear,' and 'Clairette'? A little more politeness, if you please, monsieur!" And she cut the conversation short as unceremoniously as if he had been a super.

Those who have seen Hercule only in his "act" —who think of him superb, supreme—may find it

difficult to credit the statement, but, honestly, the
Great Star used to trot at her heels like a poodle.
And she was not a beauty by any means, with her
impudent nose, and her mouth that was too big to
defy criticism. Perhaps it was her carriage that
fascinated him, the grace of her slender figure, which
he could have snapped as a child snaps jumbles.
Perhaps it was those eyes, which unwittingly promised more than she gave. Perhaps, above all, it
was her indifference. Yes, on consideration, it must
have been her indifferent air, the novelty of being
scorned, that made him a slave.

But, of course, she was more flattered by his
bondage than she showed. Every night he planted
himself in the Prompt Entrance to watch her dance
and clap his powerful hands in adulation. She could
not be insensible to the compliment, though her
smiles were oftenest for Flouflou, who planted himself, adulating, on the opposite side. *Adagio! Al-
legretto! Vivace!* Unperceived by the audience,
the gaze of the two men would meet across the
stage with misgiving. Each feared the other's attentions to her; each wished with all his heart that
the other would get the sack; they glared at each
other horribly. And, meanwhile, the orchestra
played its sweetest, and Clairette piroutted her best,
and the Public approving the obvious, saw nothing
of the intensity of the situation.

Imagine the emotions of the little juggler, jealous

by temperament, jealous even without cause, now that he beheld a giant laying siege to her affections!

And then, on a certain evening, Clairette threw but two smiles to Flouflou, and three to Hercule.

The truth is that she did not attach so much significance to the smiles as did the opponents who counted them. But that accident was momentous. The Strong Man made her a burning offer of marriage within half an hour; and next, the juggler made her furious reproaches.

Now she had rejected the Strong Man—and, coming when they did, the juggler's reproaches had a totally different effect from the one that he had intended. So far from exciting her sympathy towards him, they accentuated her compassion for Hercule. How stricken he had been by her refusal! She could not help remembering his despair as he sat huddled on the hamper, a giant that she had crushed. Flouflou was a thankless little pig, she reflected, for, as a matter of fact, he had had a good deal to do with her decision. She had deserved a better reward than to be abused by him!

Yes, her sentiments towards Hercule were newly tender, and an event of the next night intensified them. It was Hercule's custom, in every town that the "Constellation" visited, to issue a challenge. He pledged himself to present a "Purse of Gold"—it contained a ten-franc piece—to any eight men who vanquished him in a tug-of-war. The spectacle was

always an immense success—the eight yokels straining, and tumbling over one another, while Hercule,
wearing a masterful smile, kept his ten francs intact.
A tug-of-war had been arranged for the night following, and by every law of prudence, Hercule
should have abstained from the bottle during the
day.

But he did not. His misery sent discretion head-
long to the winds. Every time that he groaned for
the danseuse he took another drink, and when the
time came for him to go to the show, the giant was as
drunk as a lord. The force of habit enabled him
to fulfil some of his stereotyped performance, he
emerged from that without disgrace; but when the
eight brawny competitors lumbered on to the boards,
his heart sank. The other artists winked at one
another appreciatively, and the Manager hopped
with apprehension.

Sure enough, the hero's legs made strange trips
to-night. The sixteen arms pulled him, not only
over the chalk line, but all over the stage. They
played havoc with him. And then the Manager
had to go on and make a speech, besides, because
the "Purse of Gold" aroused dissatisfaction. The
fiasco was hideous.

"Ah, Clairette," moaned the Strong Man, pitifully, "it was all through you!"

What woman could have heard that without
emotion?

"Through me?" she murmured, faltering.

"I'm no boozer," muttered Hercule, whom the disaster had sobered. "If I took too much to-day, it was because I had got such a hump."

"But why be mashed on me, Hercule?" she pleaded; "why not think of me as a pal?"

"You're talking silly," grunted Hercule.

"Perhaps so," she confessed. "But I'm awfully sorry the show 'went' so rotten."

"Don't kid!"

"Why should I swank about it?"

"If you really meant it, you would take back what you said yesterday."

"Oh!" The gesture was dismayed.

"You see! What's the good of gassing? As soon as I ask anything of you, you dry up. Bah! I daresay you will guy me just as much as all the rest. I know you!"

"If you weren't in trouble, I'd give you a thick ear for that," she said. "You ungrateful brute!" She turned haughtily away.

"Clairette!"

"Oh, rats!"

"Don't get the needle! I'm off my rocker to-night."

"Ah!" Her hand was swift. "That's all right, cully! I've been there myself."

"Clairette?" He caught her close.

"Here, what are you at?" she cried. "Drop it!"

"Clairette?   Say 'yes.'   I'm loony about you.
There's a duck!   I'll be a daisy of a husband.   Won't
you?"

"Oh, I—I don't know," she stammered.

And thus were they betrothed.

To express what Flouflou felt would be but to
harrow the reader's sensibilities.   What he said—
rendered into English—was:

"I'd rather you had given me the go-by for any
cove in the crowd than that swine!"

They were in the ladies' dressing-room.   "The
Two Bonbons" had not finished their duet, and he
was alone with her for a moment.   She was pinning
a switch into her back hair, in front of the scrap of
looking-glass against the mildewed wall.

"You don't do yourself any good with me, Flouflou, by calling Hercule names," she replied icily.

"So he is!"

"Oh, you are jealous of him," she retorted.

"Of course I am jealous of him," owned Flouflou;
"you can't rile me by saying that!   Didn't I love you
first?   And a lump better than *he* does!"

"Now you're talking through your hat!"

"You usedn't to take any truck of him, yourself,
at the beginning.   He only got round you because
he was drunk and queered his business.   I have been
drunk, too—you didn't say you'd marry *me!*   It's
not in him to love any girl for long—he's too sweet
on himself."

"Look here," she exclaimed, "I've had enough. Hook it! And don't you speak to me any more. Understand?" She put the hairpins aside, and began to whitewash her hands and arms.

"That's the straight tip," said Flouflou, brokenly; "I'm off. Well, I wish you luck, old dear!"

"Running him down to me like that! A dirty trick, I call it."

"I never meant to, straight; I—— Sorry, Clairette!" He lingered at the door. "I suppose I shall have to say 'Madame' soon?"

"Footle!" she murmured, moved.

"You've not got your knife into me, have you, Clairette? I didn't mean to be a beast. I'd have gone to hell for you, that's all, and I wish I was dead!"

"Silly kid!" she faltered, blinking. And then "The Two Bonbons" came off to doff their costumes, and he was turned out.

Never had Hercule been so puffed up. His knowledge of the juggler's sufferings made the victory more rapturous still. No longer did Flouflou stand Opposite Prompt to watch Clairette's dance; no longer did he loiter about the passages after the curtain was down, on the chance of being permitted to escort her to her doorstep. Such privileges were the Strong Man's alone. She was affianced to him! At the swelling thought, his chest became Brobdingnagian. His bounce in company was now colossal;

and it afforded the troupe a popular entertainment
to see him drop to servility in her presence. Her
frown was sufficient to reduce him to a cringe. They
called him the "Quick-change artist."

But Hercule scarcely minded cringing to her, at
all events he scarcely minded it in a tête-à-tête; she
was unique. He would have run to her whistle, and
fawned at her kick. She had agreed to marry him
in a few weeks' time, and his head swam at the
prospect. Visions of the future dazzled him. When
he saw her to her home after the performance, he
used to talk of the joint engagements they would get
by and by—"not in 'snide' shows like this, but in
first-class halls"—and of how tremendously happy
they were going to be. And then Clairette would
stifle a sigh and say, "Oh, yes, of course!" and try
to persuade herself that she had no regrets.

Meanwhile the "Constellation" had not been playing to such good business as the Manager had an-
ticipated. He had done a bold thing in obtaining
Hercule—who, if not so famous as the posters pretended, was at least a couple of rungs above the
other humble mountebanks—and the box-office ought
to have yielded better results. M. Blond was anxious. He asked himself what the Public wanted.
Simultaneously he pondered the idea of a further
attraction, and perspired at the thought of further
expense.

At this time the "Living Statuary" turn was the

latest craze in the variety halls of fashion, and one day poor Blond, casting an expert eye on his danseuse, questioned why she should not be billed, a town or two ahead, as "Aphrodite, the Animated Statue, Direct from Paris."

To question was to act. The weather was mild, and, though Clairette experienced pangs of modesty when she learnt that the Statue's "costume" was to be applied with a sponge, she could not assert that she would be in danger of taking a chill. Besides, her salary was to be raised a trifle.

Blond rehearsed her assiduously (Madame Blond in attendance), and, to his joy she displayed a remarkable gift for adopting the poses. As "The Bather" she promised to be entrancing, and, until she wobbled, her "Nymph at the Fountain" was a pure delight. Moreover, thanks to her accomplishments as a dancer, she did not wobble very badly.

All the same, when the date of her début arrived, she was extremely nervous. Elated by his inspiration, Blond had for once been prodigal with the printing, and on her way to the stage door, it seemed to her that the name of "Aphrodite" flamed from every hoarding in the place. Hercule met her with encouraging words, but the ordeal was not one that she wished to discuss with him, and he took leave of her very much afraid that she would break down.

What was his astonishment to hear her greeted with salvos of applause! Blond's enterprise had

undoubtedly done the trick. The little hall rocked
with enthusiasm, and, cloaked in a voluminous gar-
ment, "Aphrodite" had to bow her acknowledg-
ments again and again. When the time came for
Hercule's own postures, they fell, by comparison,
quite flat.

"Ciel!" she babbled, on the homeward walk;
"who would have supposed that I should go so
strong? If I knock them like this next week too, I
shall make Blond spring a bit more!" She looked
towards her lover for congratulations; so far he
had been rather unsatisfactory.

"Oh, well," he mumbled, "it was a very good audience, you know, I never saw a more generous
house—you can't expect to catch on it like it anywhere else."

His tone puzzled her. Though she was quite alive
to the weaknesses of "the profession," she could not
believe that her triumph could give umbrage to her
fiancé. Hercule, her adorer, to be annoyed because
she had received more "hands" than *he* had? Oh,
it was mean of her to fancy such a thing!

But she was conscious that he had never wished
her "pleasant dreams" so briefly as he did that night,
and the Strong Man, on his side, was conscious of a
strange depression. He could not shake it off. The
next evening, too, he felt it. Wherever he went, he
heard praises of her proportions. The dancing girl
had, in fact, proved to be beautifully formed, and it

could not be disputed that "Aphrodite" had wiped "Hercules" out. Her success was repeated in every town. Morosely now did he make his biceps jump, and exhibit the splendours of his back—his poses commanded no more than half the admiration evoked by hers. His muscles had been surpassed by her graces. Her body had outvied his own!

Oh, she was dear to him, but he was an "artist"! There are trials that an artist cannot bear! He hesitated to refer to the subject, but when he nursed her on his lap, he thought what a great fool the Public was to prefer this ordinary woman to a marvellous man. He derived less rapture from nursing her. He eyed her critically. His devotion was cankered by resentment.

And each evening the resentment deepened. And each evening it forced him to the wings against his will. He stood watching, though every burst of approval wrung his heart. Soured, and sexless, he watched her. An intense jealousy of the slim nude figure posturing in the limelight took possession of him. It had robbed him of his plaudits. He grew to hate it, to loathe the white loveliness that had dethroned him. It was no longer the figure of a mistress that he viewed, but the figure of a rival. If he had dared, he would have hissed her.

Finally, he found it impossible to address her with civility. And Clairette married Flouflou, after all.

"Clairette," said Flouflou, on the day they were engaged, "if you don't chuck the Statuary turn, I know that one night I shall massacre the audience! Won't you give it up for me, peach?"

"So you are beginning your ructions already?" laughed Clairette. "I told you what a handful you would be! Oh, well then, just as you like, old dear —in this business a girl may meet with a worse kind of jealousy than yours!"

VII

THE CHILD IN THE GARDEN

When he reached the village of Thergrimabes at last—and after Athens the journey had been extremely trying—the curate gathered that Miss Netterville was out. As it was six months since they had met, and he had written to her that he was coming, her fiancé was vexed.

The innkeeper had laid eager hands on the portmanteau, and the traveller signed to him imperatively to put it down; "No, no," he exclaimed, "I must sleep somewhere else—if there's another inn to be found in the hole!" He remembered that it was useless to enquire for one in English. "Upon my word," his thoughts ran, "it's most annoying! Of course, we can't both lodge in the same house, and none of these peasants will understand a word I say. How very tiresome to be sure! Really, it's most inconsiderate of Gertrude to be out when I arrive! I shall have to be very firm with her; I see that I shall have to speak even more strongly than I intended!"

It was mid-day, and the sun was blazing; the

straggling white road baked under his dusty boots. The heat, and the thought that Miss Netterville would probably return to luncheon—to say nothing of the difficulty of seeking accommodation without an interpreter—decided the curate to remain for a while. "A lemon-squash," he commanded, at a venture, "bring me a lemon-squash!" And then, as the order produced only smiles and shrugs, he raised a hand to his mouth with a gesture which he felt to be rather Southern and graceful.

The landlord responded volubly, and though he brought wine instead, the Rev. Aloysius Chaysle was too thirsty and fatigued to make objections to it. He sat in a little vine-clad arbour, with the wine on a bench, and his portmanteau at his side, and was much inclined to wish that he hadn't left Bedford-shire. The situation was undignified from first to last, he felt. It was no less than three years now since Gertrude had promised to be his wife, and their marriage had been delayed by nothing but the scientific coldness of the young woman's disposition. When a girl who was betrothed to a Church of England clergyman, with private means, allowed him to pine for her in his parish while she devoted herself to the study of archæology abroad, it was time for the clergyman to put his foot down, thought Aloysius. And that was what he had travelled from Bedfordshire to do.

Meanwhile, Miss Netterville was trudging along

the road to greet him, with a frown on her intellectual brow. She was quite aware that she was
treating him unfairly, and surmised pretty shrewdly
what he had come to say, and it would all be a great
bore. The idea of marriage had never attracted
her at any time; Man—other than prehistoric—had
always been rather repellent to her than the reverse:
and she wondered why she had been weak enough
to disturb her life by becoming engaged. She approached the arbour with no enthusiasm.

"Hallo, Al!" she said; "I didn't expect you so
early. Have you been here long?"

"'I've been here the best part of an hour," replied
Aloysius. "It was disappointing to find you were
not at home. Well, how are you, Gertrude? Aren't
you going to kiss me?"

She inclined a cheek awkwardly—such physical
expressions of good feeling were distasteful to her—
and stared at the portmanteau:

"What did you bring your bag out here for?" she
asked. "Why didn't you take it upstairs?"

"Upstairs?" echoed the curate; "It must be taken
to another hotel! But I can't speak to these people
—I had to wait till you came in."

"I'm afraid that there's nothing else resembling
an hotel for miles," she said; "Thergrimabes is
rather primitive, you know."

"It seems so primitive that I'm dismayed to find
you in it; but, with all your contempt for the con-

ventions, I suppose you don't want us to be talked about? Surely you understand that it's out of the question for us both to sleep under the same roof, in the circumstances?"

"Oh, my dear Aloysius," she cried, *"please!* Spare me the artificialities! Go to one of the goatherds' cottages, if any of them has a bed to offer and you care to lie in it, but don't talk to me as if I were an ingénue in Bedfordshire—I've got beyond that sort of thing. Have they given you anything to eat? Lunch 'll be ready directly—we may as well go inside."

"Gertrude," he began strenuously, "I've something to say to you, and it's just as well to say it at once. Your letters haven't been very satisfactory— over and over again you've left a question of mine unanswered. We've been engaged for three years now, and I want you to fix a day for our wedding. Will you marry me next month?"

"Next month? Oh, no, it's impossible!"

"But why? Frankly, dear, I am losing patience. Why is it always 'impossible'? Marriage needn't interfere with your work—you can write quite as easily when we're married as you do now."

"In Bedfordshire?" she said, with a fine smile.

"I don't approve of the tone in which you mention Bedfordshire!" exclaimed Aloysius; "I presume that a book may be written in Bedfordshire as well as in Thergrimabes, or in Egypt, or any other of the remote places that you've a craze for? The whole thing is preposterous. It looks a little like affectation. It would be preposterous for a girl of twenty-eight to roam about the world unprotected, in any case——"

"Unprotected?" she echoed, "unprotected? You are talking a language that I've forgotten! Really, your notions are the most antique things in Greece!"

"I say that it would be preposterous for a young girl to roam about the world alone, in any case—you might be robbed and murdered here—and considering that you're engaged to me, it's more preposterous still. It puts me in a very false position. And it's not an easy matter to explain. People have begun to talk!"

"In Bedfordshire?" she inquired again.

"Yes, in Bedfordshire!—and they would talk in Bloomsbury, or Belgravia, or anywhere else. It's not proper, Gertrude, it is thought very improper indeed. You must remember that you are young and pretty, and——"

"Oh, don't!" she said wearily. "What an odious word! I'm not accustomed to consider my personal appearance, but I do trust that I'm not 'pretty.'"

"My sister often says that you would be extremely pretty," returned Aloysius, "if you didn't strain your hair back, and paid more attention to your clothes. But your prettiness is not the point; the main thing is our engagement—you haven't the right to behave like this, you aren't free to indulge your eccentricities, you owe a duty to Me!"

Miss Netterville lit a cigarette, and gazed thoughtfully across a mulberry tree. Characteristically, she had made no change in her costume on the day of her lover's arrival—and she had stated a fact when she declared herself indifferent to her appearance as a rule; but in spite of the ill-fitting blouse, the unbecomingly-dressed blonde hair, in spite even of the coldly intellectual eyes, she looked a desirable woman. A psychologist might have thought she looked also a woman with potentialities. But Aloysius was not a psychologist: he saw only the obvious —and not the whole of that.

"Of course I am to blame," she said at last. "I know. But then I never pretended to the kind of temperament that you admire. To me, my paramount duty must always be my work; to you, my paramount duty is to do the sort of thing that any other woman could do equally well. It is curious that I appeal to you! To be quite candid, love in its physical aspects is unpleasant to me, quite apart from the fact that marriage would be an abominable hindrance to my studies. I have no gift for domesticity; the prospect of district-visiting appals me, and tea-parties bore me to death. And I have no leaning towards maternity. I oughtn't to have promised to marry at all—I have more important things to do in my life. There are shoals of women capable of adding to the world's population, but the women capable of adding to its store of knowledge are comparatively few."

"You are expressing yourself very strangely," muttered the curate, "very strangely, indeed! If I understand you, you are breaking our engagement off."

"I don't want to be unkind," she said, "but I am quite sure that you ought to do better."

"That is a matter on which you must allow me to judge for myself—on which I did judge for myself when I proposed to you. I could certainly wish that you held more feminine views—and that you did not express the views that you do hold with such unusual bluntness—but, for good or ill, I love you. You must admit that to break off our engagement after all this time would be to treat me cruelly? I really don't know what I could say to people!"

"You could say that you had given me up—everybody would consider you were quite justified."

"I am not in the habit of telling falsehoods, Gertrude; I should have to acknowledge that you had thrown me over—at the end of three years, after I had travelled to Greece to see you; I had looked forward to a tenderer conclusion to the journey, I must say!" He, too, regarded the mulberry tree. "I—I am not unreasonable, I quite appreciate your interest in your work—archæology is a very edifying subject, I am sure, and——"

Miss Netterville made a gesture of impatience. "Please don't patronise the Ages! You mean well, but it's irritating."

"I was about to explain that if next month would be inconvenient to you on literary grounds, I would cheerfully wait until the month after," said Aloysius, with pained surprise. "Let us both make concessions—let us say in two months' time! Eh, dearest? We have both let our tongues run away with us, haven't we—both been a little hasty? What do you say? You shall share my study—you shall have your own shelves in it! Only the other day I was looking at a little bamboo desk in the High Street, and thinking how admirably it would suit you. *I'd* write my sermons while *you* wrote your book, and sometimes we might turn round and read each other what we had done. Wouldn't it be cosy now? Doesn't it sound pleasant?"

She shuddered, and nerved herself for a supreme effort:

"Al!" she stammered, "it has been a shocking mistake; I can't marry you!"

And the curate did not sleep anywhere at all in Thergrimabes—he left it the same evening. When he bade her "Good-bye," he said, "I have released you from your promise, Gertrude, because you forced me to do so; but I shan't cease to long for you, and if you ever change your mind, you must let me know. Think things over after I have gone—I shall always be hoping to hear from you." Then he climbed into the crazy vehicle, and was jolted over the white road again—a disconsolate figure beside the portmanteau that had not been unpacked—and Miss Netterville went moodily to her work.

Thergrimabes consists of its dilapidated inn and a sprinkling of hovels. Half-naked children swarm in the dust, and beg of any misguided tourist who happens to stray there from the towns beyond; goat-herds, dignified in their rags, roll cigarettes pensively, and prematurely old women occasionally appear at the doors and shade their eyes in the sun. These are the only signs of activity in Thergrimabes. For the rest, you have silence and the mountains.

Miss Netterville made many expeditions up the mountains; equipped with a scribbling block and a fountain pen, she often wrote among them. One evening—she had now written thirty thousand words, and Aloysius had been gone about a month—she heard the slow sound of hoofs. Two quaintly garbed men were riding down the track. They had evidently just observed her, and as she turned, one of them waved his sombrero to her, with an impudent smile. He was the taller of the pair, a swarthy, handsome fellow, with laughing eyes, and a big moustache that curled above full, sensual lips. She bent over her manuscript again with a frown, wondering why his glance had affected her so queerly.

The men quickened their pace, and then dis-

mounted and advanced to her. Her emotion was
pure fear; she got up, trembling.

"There is nothing to do—she is alone!" said the
smaller of the two, a weedy villain, with a squint.

"You will find you have more to do than you
think," she boasted, coolly; "I am armed."

"So you understand Greek, do you?" exclaimed
his companion. "That's all the better—I like a
girl to be able to talk to me! You are going to
have a ride with me, my beauty. If you don't come
quietly, I shall have to be rough! How is it to be?"

He learnt how it was to be at once; Miss Netterville struck at the handsome face straight from the
shoulder—throwing her body into the blow with
capital effect—and took to flight as he reeled back.
But the next instant he rushed after her; he seized
her before she had covered a dozen yards. Now
there was no chance to strike him—an arm flung
round her held her fast, and she could only scream
for help. He swung her off her feet, and stumbled
with her towards the saddle. His labouring breath
was in her face, but his eyes laughed into her own,
though the blood that she had drawn was trickling
round his mouth. As he rode off with her, crushed
against him, she could feel the heaving of his
breast under her cheek. They rode some distance
with her cheek strained against his breast before he
spoke.

"*Anathema ton!* What a spitfire you are!" he

panted. "Look what your fist has done! Don't you think you owe me a kiss for that?"

"You brute," she gasped, "I'd like to kill you!"

"You're a regular devil of a woman—I didn't know they made them like you with that coloured hair."

"You're hurting my arm," she moaned. "I can't bear it any longer!"

"Will you sit still if I don't hold so tight?"

"I couldn't escape even if I jumped off."

"That's true," said the brigand, "but I don't want the job of getting you up again; if I had your weight in gold, my dear, I'd lead an easy life!" He slackened his grasp a little, and flashed his bold, impudent smile at her—the smile that had shamed her so hotly when she first saw him. "Come, it's not disagreeable to be hugged by a man? Own up! It would be very shocking if you could help it, but you can't—remind yourself that you're not to blame, and then you can have a good time!"

"Where are you taking me?"

"To my hotel," said the facetious outlaw.

"What do you mean?"

"Call it a 'cave' if you like—I'm not proud, and I have a fancy for a quiet spot. But there's room enough for you in it—and food and wine. We'll have a bottle together. Don't look so frightened! I'll release you safe and sound when the ransom is paid, I take my oath."

Miss Netterville stared into the twilight. She might tell him that there was no one to ransom her; but if he believed the statement, he would probably be reckless how he treated her, she thought; her only safeguard was to leave him the illusion that her safety would be paid for heavily.

"How much do you demand?"

"I shall open my mouth jolly wide. You are a pretty woman—you would be very vexed if I put a low price on you!" He broke into a roar of laughter and clasped her more caressingly.

His good humour was not without a reassuring effect. The scoundrel was very human, and her horror of him had partially subsided. Indeed, as they rode on in this close embrace, she marvelled that she could bear the ignominy of it with such fortitude.

It was a long ride; her thoughts wandered in it, and curious fancies crossed her mind. She thought of Aloysius, and wished that he were different. It occurred to her that it would be pleasant to be clasped to Aloysius like this—always supposing that he were different—and then she reflected that the ride itself would be pleasant if the brigand were a gentleman, and their embrace were right. Insensibly she yielded to it more and more. It grew less repugnant to her, and even—— With a shock she realised what she had been feeling, and shivered with self-disgust.

"We have arrived," said the brigand; he carried

her inside. "It is nice to carry you, now that you don't struggle," he added.

On entering, she was plunged into darkness so intense that she could discern nothing whatever. Then she found herself borne into a cave illumined by pendant oil lamps, and furnished with considerable comfort. Beyond was a second cleft of light, and she perceived that the cave resembled a suite of rooms communicating with one another by means of apertures in the rock. The man who had assisted in her capture rejoined her now, and three others appeared, who saluted her with quiet satisfaction. There was no excitement, no hint of violence; to her surprise, her reception was as formal as if she had arrived at an inn—as formally as inn-keepers the brigands prepared to keep her prisoner.

Excepting the Captain! The Captain, as has been seen, did his business with bonhomie. If not "the mildest mannered man that ever cut a throat," at least he was the most jovial. No gallant ever filled a lady's glass, or peeled her figs with more consideration, and when he told the company how valiantly she had defended herself, he testified to her prowess with so much humour that she couldn't restrain a smile.

At the same time, it was with no little trepidation that she found herself alone with him again when the meal was finished. It proved necessary to confess that she had no friends in Greece with whom he could communicate, and, moreover, that none of her friends in England were in a position to ransom her; he twirled his moustache thoughtfully when she explained.

"No lover?" he questioned. "Rubbish, you mustn't tell me that you have no lover—a woman like you!"

"It is true," she declared.

"Nor a husband?"

"No; I was to have been married, but I changed my mind."

"*Diabole!* he had no blood in his veins, or he would have carried you off, like me! Well, it seems that I have made a bungle, eh? Women are all liars, but every man is a fool once, and I believe you! So I have had a punch in the face for nothing? That's a nice thing!"

"I have a watch on," she suggested; "you can take that if you like." It was a little Swiss watch that had cost thirty shillings. He looked at it, and gave a shrug.

"Is that what you offer me to let you go? I think you are worth more."

"I have nothing else to offer. Besides, although I haven't any friends to pay a ransom, there are plenty of people to miss me; the search might not do me much good, but it would probably end in your being shot. As you can't hope to make any money by me, you'd be wise to set me free!"

"You have brains, too, under that lovely hair," he remarked, appreciatively.   "May I offer you a cigarette?"

"No," she said; but she eyed the packet wistfully, and wished that her case were in her pocket.

"Now you are being a little donkey! Why should I wait to drug you with a cigarette when I could tap you on the head with one of these?" He touched the pistols in the sash wound round his sturdy waist. "You see I am smoking them myself—take your choice among the lot!"

Miss Netterville and the brigand smoked in silence for a few moments. Then—

"Every man is a fool once," he repeated meditatively, "but there must be a limit to his folly. If I set you free like this, what sort of ass would you think me? No better than the wooer who let you change your mind!"

"I should think you had acted like a brave and generous fellow!"

"Ah, you want to flatter me into it, you cunning cat!" he said. "Do you know that I could love you desperately, my beauty with the yellow hair? I believe I fell in love with you when I felt your fist! I like you for having hit me—I should like you to hit me again. Come and hit me again, beauty with the yellow hair—or sing me a love song! Do you sing?"

"No," she murmured.

"It's a pity, for you are a passionate woman—you would have sung well. Why did you start?"

She had started to discover that this bandit knew her better than she had known herself until an hour ago. "I didn't start," she answered.

"Fire has no heat, and there is no water in the rivers; all things are as the right woman says!" he rejoined: "So you did not start, beauty, though you have shaken the ash of your cigarette on to your knees! Well, *I* will sing to *you* instead. I will sing at your feet, while my poor comrades have only their cards to play with! It is good to be the captain sometimes—it is good to-night."

He twanged the strings, and broke into a serenade. The deep voice was untrained, but rich and sweet. After the first surprise, Miss Netterville forgot who it was that sang—it was an artist on the stage, a lover below a window; almost it was her own lover, whom she loved! The music knocked at her heart, and no trace of the smile that discomfited her so much was on the handsome face now—sentiment idealised the ruffian.

When he finished she was very pale.

"Are *you* as cold as the woman of the song?" he whispered.

"Yes," she muttered, "I *am* as cold."

"You lie," he cried; "you love me!" And the next instant she snatched a pistol from his sash—

"I'll kill myself!" she gasped.

She thought her wrist was broken as she dropped the weapon. He picked it up and paced the cave with agitation, smiting his chest, and ejaculating. Meanwhile, the English lady marvelled why she didn't loathe him.

"Will you go?" he exclaimed suddenly. "You shall go now, if you wish it; I swear you shall be guided back! I love you; I adore you; I implore you to stay! Do you wish to go?"

She bowed her head—"I wish to go."

He called to the men, and she heard their wonderment, their departing footsteps—at last the clip-clop sound of hoofs outside. All this time the captain had stood brooding silently; now he raised his head, and she saw with emotion that tears were in his eyes.

"Good-bye, *zoe mou*," he said.

"Oh!" she faltered. "Did you *really* love me then?"

He opened his arms, and Miss Netterville gave herself to them with impetuous lips.

"All is ready for the lady!" came the shout.

"They are waiting for you," said the brigand sadly.

"There—there's no hurry for a minute," Miss Netterville heard herself reply.

Before she left him he assured her that her escort might be trusted; and no mishap befell her on the road. But she had lost her nerve; a few days later she returned to England, and—perhaps she no longer considered protection so superfluous—she married Aloysius the following month, though she did not deem it necessary to inform him of her adventure.

They have been married for some years now, and get on together as well as most people. Aloysius has obtained an excellent living, and the eldest of their children is a little son, who engrosses his mother's attention to the exclusion of archæology. If it were not for her son's favourite game, the vicar's wife might think less often of her strange experience; but the boy tilts his straw hat like a sombrero, and sticks a popgun in his sash, and pretends that the summer-house is the "brigand's cave." At such times, Aloysius remarks humorously that "a little brigand is inappropriate to a vicarage garden." And the lady's eyes are wide.

VIII

THE ASSAULT IN THE RUE DES CENDRES

"Once," remarked the poet Tricotrin, pitching his pen in the air, "there were four suitors for the Most Beautiful of her Sex. The first young man was a musician, and he shut himself in his garret to create a divine melody, which should be dedicated to her. The second lover was a chemist, who experimented day and night to concoct a unique perfume, which she alone might use. The third, who was a floriculturist, aspired constantly among his bulbs to evolve a lavender rose, which should immortalise the lady's name."

"And the fourth," inquired that luckless composer, Nicholas Pitou, "what did the fourth suitor do?"

"The fourth suitor waited for her every afternoon in the sunshine, while the others were at work, and married her with great éclat. The moral of which is that, instead of cracking my head to make a sonnet to Claudine, I shall be wise to put on my hat and go to meet her."

"I rejoice that the dénouement is arrived at,"

Pitou returned, "but it would be even more absorbing if I had previously heard of Claudine."

"Miserable dullard!" cried the poet; "do you tell me that you have not previously heard of Claudine? She is the only woman I have ever loved."

"A—ah!" rejoined Pitou; "certainly, I have heard of her a thousand times—only she has never been called 'Claudine' before."

"Well, well," said Tricotrin, "we are all liable to errors of the heart. Claudine, however, represents the devotion of a lifetime! I think seriously of writing a tragedy for her to appear in."

"I shall undertake to weep copiously at it if you present me with a pass," affirmed Pitou. "She is an actress, then, this Claudine? At what theatre is she blazing—the Montmartre?"

"How often I find occasion to lament that your imagination is no larger than the Quartier! Claudine is not of Montmartre at all, at all! My poor friend, have you never heard that there are theatres on the Grands Boulevards?"

"The rumour has reached me, I confess. So, you betake yourself to haunts of fashion? Now I begin to understand why you have become so prodigal with the blacking; for some time I have had the intention of reproaching you with your shoes—our finances are not equal to such lustre."

"Ah, when one truly loves, money is no object!"

said Tricotrin. "However, if it is time mis-spent to write a sonnet to her, it is even more unprofitable to pass the evening justifying one's shoes." And, picking up his hat, the poet ran down the stairs and made his way as fast as his legs would carry him to the Comédie Moderne.

He arrived at the stage-door with no more than three minutes to spare, and disposing himself in a graceful attitude, waited for Mlle. Claudine Hillairet to come out. It might have been observed that his confidence deserted him while he waited, for, although it was perfectly true that he adored her, he had omitted to add that the passion was not mutual. He was conscious that the lady might resent his presence on the doorstep; and, in fact, when she appeared, she said nothing more tender than,

"Mon Dieu, again you! What do you want?"

"How can you ask?" sighed the poet. "I came to walk home with you lest an electric tram knocked you down at one of the crossings. What a magnificent performance you have given this evening! Superb!"

"Were you in the theatre?"

"In spirit. My spirit, which no official can exclude, is present every night, though sordid considerations force me to remain corporally in my attic. Transported by admiration, I even burst into frantic applause there. How perfect is the sympathy between our souls!"

"Listen, my boy," she said. "You are crazy, and I am sorry for your relatives, if you have any—you must be a great grief to them. But I wish you to understand that I cannot have you dangling after me and talking this bosh. What do you suppose can come of it?"

"Fame shall come of it," averred the poet, "fame for us both! Do not figure yourself that I am a dreamer. Not at all! I am practical, a man of affairs. Are you content with your position in the Comédie Moderne? No, you are not. You occupy a subordinate position; you play the rôle of a waiting-maid, which is quite unworthy of your genius, and understudy the Ingénue, who is a portly matron in robust health. The opportunity to distinguish yourself appears to you as remote as Mars. Do I romance, or is it true?"

"It is true," she said. "Well?"

"Well, I propose to alter all this—I! I have the intention of writing a great tragedy, and when it is accepted, I shall stipulate that you, and you alone, shall thrill Paris as my heroine. When the work of my brain has raised you to the pinnacle for which you were born—when the theatre echoes with our names—I shall fall at your feet, and you will murmur, 'Gustave—I love thee!' "

"Why does not your mother do something?" she asked; "is there nobody to place you where you might be cured? A tragedy? Imbecile! I am a comèdienne to the finger-tips! What should I do with your tragedy, even if it were at the Français itself?"

"You are right," said Tricotrin; "I shall turn out a brilliant comedy instead! And when the work of my brain has raised you to the pinnacle for which you were born—when the theatre echoes with our names——"

She interrupted him by a peal of laughter which disconcerted him hardly less than her annoyance.

"It is impossible to be angry with you long," she declared, "you are too comic! Also, as a friend, I do not object to you violently. Come, I advise you to be content with what you can have, instead of crying for the moon!"

"Well, I am not unwilling to make shift with it in the meantime," returned Tricotrin, "but friendship is a poor substitute for the heavens—and we shall see what we shall see. Tell me now, they mean to revive *La Curieuse* at the Comédie, I hear—what part in it have you been assigned?"

"Ah," exclaimed Mlle. Hillairet, "is it not always the same thing? I dust the same furniture with the same feather brush, and I say 'Yes,' and 'No,' and 'Here is a letter, madame.' That is all."

"I swear it is infamous!" cried the poet. "It amazes me that they fail to perceive that your gifts are buried. One would suppose that managers would know better than to condemn an artiste of esprit to perform such ignominious rôles. Also the critics! Why do not the critics call attention to an outrage which continues year by year? It appears to me that I shall have to use my influence with the Press." And so serious was the tone in which he made this boast, that the fair Claudine began to wonder if she had after all underrated the position of her out-at-elbows gallant.

"Your influence?" she questioned, with an eager smile. "Have you, then, influence with the critics?"

"We shall see what we shall see," repeated Tricotrin, significantly. "I am not unknown in Paris, and I have your cause at heart—I may make a star of you yet. But while we are on the subject of astronomy, one question! When my services have transformed you to a star, shall I still be compelled to cry for the moon?"

Mlle. Hillairet's tones quivered with emotion as she murmured how grateful to him she would be, and it was understood, when he took leave of her, that if he indeed accomplished his design, his suit would be no longer hopeless.

The poet pressed her hand ardently, and turned homeward in high feather; and it was not until he had trudged a mile or so that the rapture in his soul began to subside under the remembrance that he had been talking through his hat.

"In fact," he admitted to Pitou when the garret was reached, "my imagination took wings unto itself; I am committed to a task beside which the labours of Hercule were as child's play. The question now arises how this thing, of which I spoke so confidently, is to be effected. What do you suggest?"

"I suggest that you allow me to sleep," replied Pitou, "for I shall feel less hungry then."

"Your suggestion will not advance us," demurred Tricotrin. "We shall, on the contrary, examine the situation in all its bearings. Listen! Claudine is to enact the waiting-maid in *La Curieuse*, which will be revived at the Comédie Moderne in a fortnight's time; she will dust the Empire furniture, and say 'Yes' and 'No' with all the intellect and animation for which those monosyllables provide an opening. Have you grasped the synopsis so far? Good! On the strength of this performance, it has to be stated by the foremost dramatic critic in Paris that she is an actress of genius. Now, how is it to be done? How shall we induce Labarregue to write of her with an outburst of enthusiasm in *La Voix*?"

"Labarregue?" faltered Pitou. "I declare the audacity of your notion wakes me up!"

"Capital," said Tricotrin, "we are making progress already! Yes, we must have Labarregue—it has never been my custom to do things by halves. Dramatically, of course, I should hold a compromising paper of Labarregue's. I should say, 'Monsieur, the price of this document is an act of justice

to Mlle. Claudine Hillairet. It is agreed? **Good!**
Sit down—you will write from my dictation!' "

"However——" said Pitou.

"However—I anticipate your objection—I do not
hold such a paper. Therefore, that scene is cut.
Well, let us find another! Where is your fertility
of resource? Mon Dieu! Why should I speak to
him at all?"

"I do not figure myself that you will speak to him
—you would never get the chance."

"Precisely my own suspicion. What follows?
Instead of wasting my time seeking an interview
which would not be granted——"

"And which would lead to nothing even if it were
granted!"

"And which would lead to nothing even if it were
granted, as you point out; instead of doing this, it
is evident that I must write Labarregue's criticism
myself!"

"Hein?" ejaculated Pitou, sitting up in bed.

"I confess that I do not perceive yet how it is to
be managed, but obviously it is the only course.
I must write what is to be said, and *La Voix* must
believe that it has been written by Labarregue!
Come, we are getting on famously—we have now
decided what we are to avoid!"

"By D'Artagnan, Athos, Porthos, and Aramis,"
cried Pitou, "this will be the doughtiest adventure in
which we have engaged!"

"You are right, it is an adventure worthy of our steel—by which I mean our steel pens. We shall enlighten the public, crown an artiste, and win her heart by way of reward—that is to say, *I* shall win her heart by way of reward. What your own share of the booty will be I do not recognise, but I promise you, at least, a generous half of the dangers."

"My comrade!" murmured Pitou; "Ever loyal! But do you not think that *La Voix* will smell a rat? What about the handwriting?"

"It is a weak point which had already presented itself to me. Could I have constructed the situation to my liking, Labarregue would have the custom to typewrite his notices; however, as he is so inconsiderate as to knock them off in the Café de l'Europe, he has not that custom, and we must adapt ourselves to the circumstances that exist. The probability is that a criticism delivered by the accredited messenger, and signed with the familiar 'J. L.' will be passed without question; the difference in the handwriting may be attributed to an amanuensis. When the great man writes his next notice, I shall make it my business to be taking a bock in the Café de l'Europe, in order that I may observe closely what happens. There is to be a répétition générale at the Vaudeville on Monday night—on Monday night, therefore, I hope to advise you of our plan of campaign. Now do not speak to me any more—I am about to compose a eulogy on

Claudine, for which Labarregue will, in due course, receive the credit."

The poet fell asleep at last, murmuring dithyrambic phrases; and if you suppose that in the soberness of daylight he renounced his harebrained project, it is certain that you have never lived with Tricotrin in Montmartre.

No, indeed, he did not renounce it. On Monday night—or rather in the small hours of Tuesday morning—he awoke Pitou with enthusiasm.

"Mon vieux," he exclaimed, "the evening has been well spent! I have observed, and I have reflected. When he quitted the Vaudeville, Labarregue has entered the Café de l'Europe, seated himself at his favourite table, and written without cessation for half an hour. When his critique was finished, he placed it in an envelope, and commanded his supper. All this time I, sipping a bock leisurely, have accorded to his actions a scrutiny worthy of the secret police. Presently a lad from the office of *La Voix* has appeared; he approached Labarregue, received the envelope, and departed. At this point, my bock was finished; I paid for it and sauntered out, keeping the boy well in view. His route to the office lay through a dozen streets which were all deserted at so late an hour; but I remarked one that was even more forbidding than the rest—a mere alley that seemed positively to have been designed for our purpose. Our course is clear—we shall attack him in the Rue des Cendres."

"Really?" inquired Pitou, somewhat startled.

"But really! We will not shed his blood; we will make him turn out his pockets, and then, disgusted by the smallness of the swag, toss it back to him with a cuff on the ear. Needless to say that when he escapes, he will be the bearer of *my* criticism, not of Labarregue's. He will have been too frightened to remark the exchange."

"It is not bad, your plan."

"It is an inspiration! But to render it absolutely safe, we must have an accomplice."

"Why, is he so powerful, your boy?"

"No, mon ami, the boy is not so powerful, but the alley has two ends—I do not desire to be arrested while I am giving a life-like representation of an Apache. I think we will admit Lajeunie to our scheme—as a novelist he should appreciate the situation. If Lajeunie keeps guard at one end of the alley, while you stand at the other, I can do the business without risk of being interrupted and removed to gaol."

"It is true. As a danger signal, I shall whistle the first bars of my Fugue."

"Good! And we will also arrange a signal with Lajeunie. Mon Dieu! will not Claudine be amazed next day? I shall not breathe a word to her in the meantime; I shall let her open *La Voix* without expectation; and then—ah, what joy will be hers! 'The success of the evening was made by the actress who took the rôle of the maid-servant, and who had perhaps six words to utter. But with what vivacity, with what esprit were they delivered! Every gesture, every sparkle of the eyes, betokened the comédienne. For myself, I ceased to regard the fatuous Ingénue, I forgot the presence of the famous Leading lady; I watched, absorbed, the facial play of this maid-servant, whose brains and beauty, I predict, will speedily bring Paris to her feet!' "

"Is that what you mean to write?"

"I shall improve upon it. I am constantly improving—that is why the notice is still unfinished. It hampers me that I must compose in the strain of Labarregue himself, instead of allowing my eloquence to soar. By the way, we had better speak to Lajeunie on the subject soon, lest he should pretend that he has another engagement for that night; he is a good boy, Lajeunie, but he always pretends that he has engagements in fashionable circles."

The pair went to him the following day, and when they had climbed to his garret on the sixth floor, found the young literary man in bed.

"It shocks me," said Pitou, "to perceive that you rise so late, Lajeunie; why are you not dashing off chapters of a romance?"

"Mon Dieu," replied Lajeunie, "I was making studies among the beau monde until a late hour last night at a reception; and, to complete my fatigue, it was impossible to get a cab when I left."

"Naturally; it happens to everybody when he lacks a cab-fare," said Tricotrin. "Now tell me, have you any invitation from a duchess for next Thursday evening?"

"Thursday, Thursday?" repeated Lajeunie, thoughtfully. "No, I believe that I am free for Thursday."

"Now, that is fortunate!" exclaimed Tricotrin. "Well, we want you to join us on that evening, my friend."

"Indeed, we should be most disappointed otherwise," put in Pitou.

"Certainly; I shall have much pleasure," said Lajeunie. "Is it a supper?"

"No," said Tricotrin, "it is a robbery. I shall explain. Doubtless you know the name of 'Mademoiselle Claudine Hillairet'?"

"Never heard it in my life. Is she in Society?"

"Society? She is in the Comédie Moderne. She is a great actress, but—like us all—unrecognised."

"My heart bleeds for her. Another comrade!"

"I was sure I could depend upon your sympathy. Well, on Thursday night they will revive *La Curieuse* at the Comédie, and I myself propose to write Jules Labarregue's critique of the performance. Do you tumble?"

"It is a gallant action. Yes, I grasp the climax,

but at present I do not perceive how the plot is to be constructed."

"Labarregue's notices are despatched by messenger," began Pitou.

"From the Café de l'Europe," added Tricotrin.

"So much I know," said Lajeunie.

"I shall attack the messenger, and make a slight exchange of manuscripts," Tricotrin went on.

"A blunder!" proclaimed Lajeunie; "you show a lack of invention. Now be guided by me, because I am a novelist and I understand these things. The messenger is an escaped convict, and you say to him, 'I know your secret. You do my bidding, or you go back to the galleys; I shall give you three minutes to decide!' You stand before him, stern, dominant, inexorable—your watch in your hand."

"It is at the pawn-shop."

"Well, well, of course it is; since when have you joined the realists? Somebody else's watch— or a clock. Are there no clocks in Paris? You say, 'I shall give you until the clock strikes the hour.' That is even more literary—you obtain the solemn note of the clock to mark the crisis."

"But there is no convict," demurred Tricotrin; "there are clocks, but there is no convict."

"No convict? The messenger is not a convict?"

"Not at all—he is an apple-cheeked boy."

"Oh, it is a stupid plot," said Lajeunie, "I shall not collaborate in it!"

"Consider!" cried Tricotrin; "do not throw away the chance of a lifetime—think what I offer you! You shall hang about the end of a dark alley, and whistle if anybody comes. How literary again is that! You may develop it into a novel that will make you celebrated! Pitou will be at the other end; I and the apple-cheeked boy who is to die— that is to say, to be duped—will occupy the centre of the stage—I mean the middle of the alley. And on the morrow, when all Paris rings with the fame of Claudine Hillairet, I, who adore her, shall have won her heart!"

"Humph," said Lajeunie. "Well, since the synopsis has a happy ending, I consent. But I make one condition—I must wear a crêpe mask! Without a crêpe mask I perceive no thrill in my rôle."

"Madness!" objected Pitou. "Now listen to *me* —I am serious-minded, and do not commit follies, like you fellows. A crêpe mask will arouse attention —it is not an ordinary object in a thoroughfare. Believe me, if you loiter at the corner of a street with a crêpe mask on, any passer-by will regard you, may even wonder what you are doing there. It might ruin the whole job."

"Pitou is right," announced Tricotrin, after profound consideration.

"Well, then," said Lajeunie, "*you* must wear a crêpe mask! Put it on when you attack the boy.

I have always had a passion for crêpe masks, and this is the first opportunity that I find to gratify it. I insist that somebody wears a crêpe mask, or I wash my hands of the conspiracy."

"I!" assented Tricotrin. "In the alley it will do no harm; indeed it will prevent the boy identifying me. Good, on Thursday night then! In the meantime we shall rehearse the crime assiduously, and you and Pitou can practise your whistles. It is agreed."

With what diligence did the poet write each day now! How lovingly he selected his superlatives! Never in the history of the Press had such ardent care been lavished on a criticism—truly it was not until Thursday afternoon that he was satisfied that he could do no more. He put the pages in his pocket, and, too impatient even to be hungry, roamed about the Quartier, reciting to himself the most hyperbolic of his periods.

And dusk gathered over Paris, and the lights sprang out, and the tense hours crept away.

It was precisely half-past eleven when the three conspirators arrived at the doors of the Comédie Moderne, and lingered near by until the audience poured forth. Labarregue was among the first to appear. He paused on the steps to take a cigarette, and stepped briskly into the noise and glitter of the boulevard. The young men followed, exchanging feverish glances. Soon the glow of the Café de l'Europe was visible. The critic entered, made a sign to a waiter, and seated himself gravely at a table.

Everybody gazed at him with interest. To those who did not know, habitués whispered, "There is Labarregue—see, he comes to write his criticism on the revival of *La Curieuse!*" Labarregue affected unconsciousness of all this, but secretly he lapped it up. Occasionally he passed his hand across his brow with a gesture profoundly intellectual.

Few people remarked that at brief intervals three shabby young men strolled in, who betrayed no knowledge of one another, and merely called for bocks. None suspected that these humble customers plotted to consign the celebrity's criticism to the flames.

Without a sign of recognition, taciturn and impassive, the three young men waited, their eyes bent upon the critic's movements.

By and by Labarregue thrust his "copy" into an envelope that was provided. Some moments afterwards one of the young men asked another waiter for the materials to write a letter. The paper he crumpled in his pocket; in the envelope he placed the forged critique.

A quarter of an hour passed. Then a youth of about sixteen hurried in and made his way to Labarregue's table. At this instant Lajeunie rose and left. As the youth received the "copy," Tricotrin also sauntered out. When the youth again reached the door, it was just swinging behind Pitou.

The conspirators were now in the right order— Lajeunie pressing forward, Tricotrin keeping pace with the boy, Pitou a few yards in the rear.

The boy proceeded swiftly. It was late, and even the Grands Boulevards showed few pedestrians now; in the side streets the quietude was unbroken. Tricotrin whipped on his mask at the opening of the passage. When the messenger was half-way through it, the attack was made suddenly, with determination.

"Fat one," exclaimed the poet, "I starve—give me five francs!"

"Hein?" stammered the youth, jumping; "I have not five francs, I!"

"Give me all you have—empty your pockets, let me see! If you obey, I shall not harm you; if you resist, you are a dead boy!"

The youth produced, with trepidation, a sou, some cigarettes, a piece of string, a clasp knife, a young lady's photograph, and Labarregue's notice. The next moment the exchange of manuscripts had been deftly accomplished.

"Devil take your rubbish," cried the Apache; "I want none of it—there! Be off, or I shall shoot you for wasting my time."

The whole affair had occupied less than a minute; and the three adventurers skipped to Montmartre rejoicing.

And how glorious was their jubilation in the hour when they opened *La Voix* and read Tricotrin's pronouncement over the initials "J. L."! There it was, printed word for word—the Leading lady was dismissed with a line, the Ingénue received a sneer, and for the rest, the column was a panegyric of the waiting-maid! The triumph of the waiting-maid was unprecedented and supreme. Certainly, when Labarregue saw the paper, he flung round to the office furious; but *La Voix* did not desire people to know that it had been taken in, so the matter was hushed up, and Labarregue went about pretending that he actually thought all those fine things of the waiting-maid.

The only misfortune was that when Tricotrin called victoriously upon Claudine, to clasp her in his arms, he found her in hysterics on the sofa—and it transpired that she had not represented the waiting-maid after all. On the contrary, she had at the last moment been promoted to the part of the Ingénue, while the waiting-maid had been played by a little actress whom she much disliked.

"It is cruel, it is monstrous, it is heartrending!" gasped Tricotrin, when he grasped the enormity of his failure; "but, light of my life, why should you blame *me* for this villainy of Labarregue's?"

"I do not know," she said; "however, you bore me, you and your 'influence with the Press.' Get out!"

IX

HERBERT HARDING was one of the most distinguished dramatic critics in London, one of the most scholarly and acute. Yet no man is a prophet to his family, and at home "H. H." was considered to be "wasting his life at the game."

Of course, the old people took the paper in which his first-night notices appeared, and they wrestled with his essays in volume form—essays, by the way, which will always be ranked among the most valuable contributions to the psychology of the theatre—but the references to Diderot, and Stendhal, and other people of whom they had never heard before baffled them mightily, and if the book had been written by anybody but Herbert, they would never have read a dozen pages of it. As Harding senior, a sensible and hearty Englishman, used to say to his wife, "Thank God, he wasn't literary himself, and to discuss whether the heroine of a play would have behaved like this, or have behaved like that, when one knew that she wasn't a real woman at all, seemed to him the sort of tomfoolishness for young girls in a

138

drawing-room, and not the kind of thing he would have expected a son of his to do for a living, damn it!"

There were persons who professed to see in the fact that Harding had always been unappreciated by his relatives, the explanation of his marriage. But there were many cultured women who admired him; Gertrude Millington's homage was not singular. She was, certainly, amiable, and she "wrote"; yet when one remembers the triviality of her stories, one would have supposed her authorship would deter, rather than attract, a man like Harding. Besides, he had privately resented the necessity for making her acquaintance.

She was a friend of one of his sisters—he had met her when he went down to his people for a fortnight in the autumn—and his mother had said:

"Oh, my son Herbert—Miss Millington. You have often heard us talk of Miss Millington, Herbert? You two should find lots to say to each other, both being writers."

Harding, who had never heard Miss Millington's name till then, there or anywhere else, thought that his mother ought to have known better.

Perhaps the girl thought so, too, for her smile was embarrassed.

"I never expected to get the chance to meet Mr. Harding," she said reverentially.

Harding thawed. Since she recognised him as a

master, he was prepared to tolerate her. In five minutes he had gathered that to be talking to him was one of the events of her life.

Naturally they talked of the theatre, and though her attitude towards the drama was untrained, Harding perceived an eagerness to be enlightened, a quickness of intelligence that saved him from being bored. That, at any rate, was how he put it to himself, though whether her eagerness and intelligence would have interested him if she had not been passably good-looking is a doubtful point.

The fortnight proved uncommonly pleasant to him, and as he did not have an opportunity for looking at any of her work until they were back in town and he was well in love with her, the crudity of her fiction did not infuriate him so violently as it would have done otherwise. On the contrary, he persuaded himself that, underlying the immaturities of style and characterisation, there was the glint of genuine talent.

His income, derived solely from his pen, was slender; but everything is relative, and Miss Millington lived in a boarding-house in West Kensington. Compared with her own, his means were substantial. To cut the courtship short, he married her. Miss Millington, the unknown, became the wife of Harding, the august. Women who had made a reputation called on them, and "wondered what he could have seen in her, they were sure!" His best friends

confessed themselves "a bit surprised at his choice";
and Harding, with all the ardour of his intellect and
his affection, proceeded to cultivate his wife's mind.

Never was a disciple more devoted. She put her
story-writing aside—he had advised her to do that
until she was more widely read—and plodded con-
scientiously through the list of classics that he drew
up for her improvement. As often as he obtained
two seats, she went to the theatre with him, and
listened absorbed to his catalogue of the play's de-
fects. Because she loved him dearly and panted to
please, she never failed to assure him that she understood, and thoroughly agreed with everything he
said—though this was a flagrant lie—and Harding
promoted her to Ibsen, and expounded his qualities
to her for hours on end.

She grew to miss her scribbling by degrees. By
degrees she grew to sicken at the intellectual stuffing.
Before long, her delight at going to a theatre was
marred by her dread of the critic's edifying mono-
logue when they returned. But she never yawned,
she never faltered—she endured the deadly dulness
of her education without a murmur.

Her confinement was a holiday. Harding, however, was far too fond of his wife to neglect her because he had a son, and after she was up again, he
devoted as much earnest attention to her as before.
By this time she could give forth dozens of his
opinions with all the fidelity of a phonograph, and

he contemplated her progress with the tenderest pride.

The baby, and a nurse, and the necessary change in the domestic arrangements meant increased expenses, and now she sometimes reflected that the modest cheques obtainable by her pen would be an aid.

Once she said to him:

"Herbert, when do you think I might go back to my work? Don't you think I might write something again now?"

"What do you want to write?" he asked, with an indulgent smile.

"I suppose what I ought to do is another book; I should like to write a play, though."

"A play?" He stared. "My child, you aren't a dramatist."

"Well, I never shall be one if I don't make a beginning. I should think I ought to be able to manage a piece, after all I've read."

Harding smiled again, wryly. The temerity of the novice was a wonderful thing.

"You know more than you did, but dramatic construction isn't to be mastered in a year and a half, goose, even by the born playwright."

"It's never to be mastered at all without trying, is it?"

There was a touch of obstinacy in her tone, and he was greatly disappointed. Since she could speak in so light a fashion of accomplishing a play, it seemed that she had learnt nothing, after all. The magnitude of the undertaking did not impress her in the least—she talked like the proverbial amateur.

"Doesn't it occur to you," he said patiently, "that, although I know considerably more about it than you do, *I* don't write plays? I recognise what I lack. And I recognise what *you* lack. I'm not trying to make a dramatist of you, my child—I simply want you to have an acquaintance with what is best in dramatic literature, I want you to be able to discriminate. As to your writing again, perhaps you will. But not yet. Not yet, by any means! And when you do, of course it should be a story. Really whether you write, or whether you don't, is of no importance—why aspire to authorship?"

Before they married she had counted herself an author already. She winced. But his remonstrance, affectionate as it was, took the pluck out of her. She let the subject drop, and put her aspirations on the shelf. She divided her time between the baby and the books henceforth, though the baby came gradually to receive the larger share.

They had three children, and an odious little house in Balham when she did pencil "Act I.—A Drawing Room" at last. She did not mean to let Harding guess her project till the comedy was finished. She knew that he would have discouraged her, that he would have repeated that she had no qualifications

for dramatic work, or, at best, that it was years too
soon for her to attempt it. But she told herself that
when the piece was done, when she read it to him,
and saw his pleasure, that would make amends for
everything. She pictured his surprise as she said
carelessly, "Oh, by the way, if you can spare an hour
this evening, there's something I want you to hear!"
The anxiety of his gaze as she produced the manuscript and announced "A Comedy in Three Acts," she
could imagine that too! He would sit down nervously, twisting his moustache, and, of course, her
voice would wobble frightfully. Then presently his
face would change—she foresaw his smile, the sudden lift of his head at a good line, the growing
wonder of his expression. In her hopes she heard
him exclaim that her work had wit, brilliance, and,
above all, reality—that she had amazed and made
him proud of her. It was a young and rather foolish
woman's dream, but it sprang from her love for him
quite as much as from her personal ambitions.

And she wrote. She drove her pen in secret for
months, not that she was a slow writer—far from it
—but there were few occasions on which she could
feel confident of being undisturbed. Her best hours
were when there was a "first night" somewhere, for
then there was no danger of Harding popping into
the room before she could thrust the manuscript out
of sight. While the critic sat in judgment at the
theatre, his wife sat in Balham scribbling dialogue

with a rapidity that would have horrified him. Indeed, it made her distrust herself in moments; she questioned if it was possible for first-rate work to be produced so quickly. Yet when she read the scene, it sounded capital. She came to the conclusion that her swiftness proved her to be even more accomplished as a dramatist than she had supposed. Harding generally found her in high good-humour when he returned. And, though it was very late, for his notice had to be delivered before he came back, he used to tell her the plot of the play that he had been to see, and she would agree sapiently with all his observations.

The disciple had, in fact, become a companion by now, and, despite the state of the exchequer, Harding knew no regret for having married her. When he recalled the uncultured girl of the honeymoon, and contrasted her with the woman who understood most of his English references and quotations, he was delighted with the success he had effected. It was with a shock, a shudder, one day, that he picked off the mantel-piece a bill for typewriting *"The Audacity of Dinah,* in three acts." Forebodings hinted that his success wasn't quite so triumphant as he had thought.

"What's this?"

"Oh!" How stupid she had been to leave it there! Now she had to tell him the great news differently from the way she had planned. "It's mine."

"I see it is," said Harding. *"The Audacity of Dinah?"*

Her nod was embarrassed. "Yes."

"I didn't know you were writing."

"No, I didn't want you to know till I could read it to you; I meant to tell you after dinner, I—I'm very anxious to hear if you think it will do." She flushed, and smiled shyly. "I'm rather pleased with it; I've been at it a long time; I think—I think I've done something you'll find a good word for."

"Baby!" said Harding, pinching her cheek; "I've no doubt I shall find a good word for it, but I'm afraid I shall have to say things you won't like, too. I shall be quite candid with you, I warn you!"

"Oh, that's just what I want," she declared, laughing happily; "I want you to forget who I am altogether—you must be just Herbert Harding listening to a new author. No compliments, no—what's the word?—euphemisms! It's to be real criticism, please!"

"All right," he said. "Well, when am I to hear it—at once?"

"I think after dinner will be best—I've always pictured you listening to it after dinner. And there'll be nothing to interrupt us when the last post has been. Mind, I shall be awfully frightened; you must make allowances for that."

Something in her bearing, in her voice—more still, perhaps, something in the fact that she was dear to him—raised his hopes. His suspense was nearly as keen as her own while they dined. And when the servant had shut the door, and Gertrude commanded him to "sit down in that chair," and to refrain from looking at her for the first few minutes, his hands were not quite steady as he filled his pipe.

She drew her own chair to the table, and after an instant's hesitation, began to read.

Harding listened intently, his gaze fixed on the fire. And before she had read for half an hour astonishment laid hold of him. Awhile ago, catching something of her excitement, he had fancied that the play might reveal a talent that he had under-rated, a promise of good things to come; originally, he had fancied that it would repel him; but at no time had he fancied that it would be quite so dejecting as it was. He was astounded that any woman who had studied so much good work could be capable of writing so badly. The man suffered—silently and acutely suffered—as, gaining courage, she declaimed her travesty of human nature with gusto. He pitied her, he could have wept for her, he would rather have been compelled to sit out a pantomime every night for a year than to tell her the truth.

But she closed the covers of Act I., and said, with her soul in her eyes, "Well?"

He shifted the pipe between his teeth, and stifled a groan. "Let me hear it right through," he answered, postponing the evil moment.

"Act II.," she continued in a clear voice.

It was eleven o'clock when the ordeal ended. His wife leant back in her seat, her hands clasped in her lap, and waited.

Despairingly he sought for some particle of honest praise.

"The theme isn't bad," he said.

"Ah!"

"But it isn't worked out properly."

"Oh!"

He hastened to add, "There are lots of very pretty lines."

"That's nice!" She beamed.

"You put them in the wrong people's mouths, though. In the last act, you make your misanthrope talk like the Cheeryble Brothers."

"Kindness has changed his nature then. Don't you like the girl?"

"She's not consistent," he complained; "she's seventeen one minute, and thirty-five the next. She has had 'no social experience,' yet she scores off the woman of the world in every answer. That's the fault all through—if you see a chance for something smart, you can't resist it, whether it's appropriate to the character or not. The mother makes an epigram in the situation where she thinks her son has been killed—she'd be inarticulate, she wouldn't fire off epigrams."

There was a long pause. At last she said, stonily:

"In other words you don't think anything of it?"
He shifted the pipe again. "Well——"

"Oh, be frank, Herbert!" she cried. She was very
white. "There mustn't be any humbug between you
and me!"

"It's no good, Gertie," he confessed wretchedly.

She gathered it up, and put it in a drawer, and shut
the drawer very quietly. Her mouth had hardened.
He was a distinguished critic, and her husband; but
she was an author, and her pride was in arms. For
the first time she doubted his wisdom. For the first
time she opposed her will to his. It was "no good,"
he had said—she could not accept the pronouncement, she would prove to him that he was wrong!

"We won't talk any more about it," she said presently, when he offered some feeble comfort. "I've
made a mistake, that's all." But she meant that her
mistake was having invited his opinion, not having
written the comedy.

She determined to submit it to the Piccadilly
Theatre without delay. Of course, she would not
put her own name to it now—as he thought it so
worthless he would probably object to its being known
as his wife's even if it were produced. She would
choose a pseudonym. And if her work were taken,
if it made a success, she would mention to him, very
gently, but firmly, that he was too ready to find fault,
that his prejudices warped his judgment—in fact,

that he wasn't quite so excellent a critic as he believed himself to be.

At this point it may be stated that his criticism of *The Audacity of Dinah* was absolutely sound. The piece was every bit as bad as he thought it.

She posted the manuscript the following afternoon, and many weeks later it was returned to her with "regret." The Piccadilly, she said doggedly, was not the only theatre in London—she made up the parcel once more and sent it to the Diadem. The Diadem also "regretted," and took longer to communicate the fact. To several West-End theatres the comedy was offered unavailingly; and then—she re-read the brief note with rapture several times—a manager wrote asking her to call.

Not before the contract was signed and stamped did she announce her news to Harding. It was a great moment for her. Nearly eighteen months had passed since the day of the reading, but she had not forgotten the humiliation that he had inflicted. He realised that suddenly, discomfitingly, by the inflections of her voice, by the look in her eyes, by her new air of self-esteem.

"I'm very glad for you," he faltered. And she replied, "I'm sure you are, dear," with a touch of patronage.

He did not attend the production himself; as he explained to her, he would have been bound to express his convictions sincerely. The Editor put on another man to "do" *The Audacity of Dinah,* and, on the whole, the other man's notice was favourable. With a few exceptions, all the Press was tolerant. Better still, the piece captured the Public. The booking next day was brisk, and increased steadily through the week. On the second Saturday night they played to "the capacity of the house." The comedy came to be known as one of the few genuine successes of the year, and of course it had leaked out that the author was Mrs. Herbert Harding. The illustrated journals devoted a page to her photograph, favouring their readers with details of her "literary methods," and with her views on the world in general. A manufacturer's advertisements informed the kingdom that *The Audacity of Dinah* had been written with a "Dashaway Fountain Pen (price 10s. 6d., of all stationers)." She lectured to the Front Row Club on "How to Write a Play." Posters proclaimed the "300th Performance." And various theatrical managers expressed a deferential hope that they, too, might be privileged to produce some of her brilliant work.

They were. She has never written anything so popular since, but she has reeled out several successful plays, of similar quality. The Hardings have removed from Balham, and live in a high-sounding Terrace at a fashionable Gate, and the children often caution Herbert "not to make a noise on the stairs, because mamma is busy." Gertrude is a personage who speaks with quiet authority in the home to-day, and drives to rehearsal in a thousand-guinea motor-car. When he goes alone, the critic takes an omnibus, and feels more cheerful. In spite of the luxurious ménage that she provides, he wishes frequently that he were alone for good.

X

AN INVITATION TO DINNER

ONE summer, the creators of Eau d'Enfer invited designs for a poster calling the attention of the world to their liqueur's incomparable qualities. It occurred to Théodose Goujaud that this was a first-class opportunity to demonstrate his genius.

For an article with such a glistering name it was obvious that a poster must be flamboyante—one could not advertise a "Water of Hell" by a picture of a village maiden plucking cowslips—and Goujaud passed wakeful nights devising a sketch worthy of the subject. He decided at last upon a radiant brunette sharing a bottle of the liqueur with his Satanic Majesty while she sat on his knee.

But where was the girl to be found? Though his acquaintance with the models of Paris was extensive, he could think of none with a face to satisfy him. Susanne's arms wreathed themselves before his mind, Isabelle's feet were desirable, but the face, which was of supreme importance, eluded his most frenzied search. "Mon Dieu," groaned Goujaud, "here I am projecting a poster that would conquer

Paris, and my scheme is frustrated by the fact that Nature fails to produce women equal to the heights of my art! It is such misfortunes as this that support the Morgue."

"I recommend you to travel," said Gustave Tricotrin, the poet; "a tour in the East might yield your heart's desire."

"It's a valuable suggestion," rejoined Goujaud; "I should also like a couple of new shirts, but I lack the money to acquire them."

"Well," said Tricotrin, "the Salle de Belleville is nearer. Try that!"

Goujaud looked puzzled. "The Salle de Belleville?" he repeated; "I do not know any Salle de Belleville."

"Is it possible?" cried the poet; "where do you live? The Salle de Belleville, my recluse, is positively the most fascinating resort in Paris. I have been familiar with it for fully a week. It is where the criminal classes enjoy their well-earned leisure. Every Saturday night they frisk at a ball. The Cutthroats' Quadrille is a particularly sprightly measure, and the damsels there are often striking."

"And their escorts, too, no doubt—if an Apache planted his knife in my bosom it might curtail my career."

"In the interests of art," replied Tricotrin, "one must incur some slight inconvenience. Come, if you are in earnest, I will introduce you to the place, and

give you a few hints. For example, the company
have a prejudice against collars, and, assuming for
a moment that you possessed more than a franc, you
would do well to leave the surplus at home."

Goujaud expanded his chest.

"As a matter of fact," he announced languidly,
"I possess five hundred francs." And so dignified
was his air that Tricotrin came near to believing
him.

"You possess five hundred francs? You? How?
No, such things do not occur! Besides, you mentioned a moment since that you were short of shirts."

"It is true that I am short of shirts," answered
Goujaud, "but, nevertheless, I have five hundred
francs in my pocket. It is like this. My father, who
is not artistic, has always desired to see me renounce
my profession and sink to commerce. Well, I was at
the point of yielding—man cannot live by hope
alone, and my pictures were strangely unappreciated.
Then, while consent trembled on my lips, up popped
this Eau d'Enfer! I saw my opportunity, I recognised that, of all men in Paris, I was the best
qualified to execute the poster. You may divine the
sequel. I addressed my father with burning eloquence, I persuaded him to supply me with the means
to wield my brush for a few months longer. If my
poster succeeds, I become a celebrity. If it fails, I
become a pétrole-merchant. The coming months
decide my fate. In the meanwhile I am a capitalist,

but it would be madness for me to purchase shirts, for I shall require every sou to support existence until the poster is acclaimed."

"You have a practical head!" exclaimed Tricotrin admiringly; "I foresee that you will go far. Let us trust that the Salle de Belleville will prove the ante-chamber to your immortality."

"I have no faith in your Salle de Belleville," de-murred the painter; "the criminal classes are not keen on sitting for their portraits—the process has unpleasant associations to them. Think again! I can spare half an hour this morning. Evolve a further inspiration on the subject!"

"Do you imagine I have nothing to do but to provide you with a model? My time is fully occu-pied; I am engaged upon a mystical play, which is to be called 'The Spinster's Prayer; or, The Goblin Child's Mother,' and take Paris by storm. À propos —yes, now I come to think of it, there is something in that journal that might suit you."

"My preserver!" returned Goujaud. "What it it?"

Tricotrin picked it up and read:

"WANTED: A HUNDRED LADIES FOR THE STAGE.—Beauty more essential than talent. No dilapidations need apply. Lavalette's Dramatic Agency, Rue Baba, Thursday, 12 to 5."

"Mon Dieu! Now you are beginning to talk," said Goujaud. "A hundred! One among them

should be suitable, hein?   But, all the same——"
He hesitated.   " 'Twelve to five' means five hours.
It will be tedious, standing on a doorstep for five
hours, especially if the rain streams."

"Do you expect a Cleopatra to call at your attic,
or to send an eighty horse-power motor car, that you
may cast your eye over her?   Anyhow, there may be
a café opposite; you can order a bock on the terrace,
and make it last."

"You are right," assented the painter; "I shall go
and inspect the spot at once.   A hundred beauties!
I declare the advertisement might have been framed
to meet my wants.   How fortunate that you chanced
to see it!   To-morrow evening you shall hear
the result—dine with me at the Faisan d'Or at eight
o'clock.   For one occasion I undertake to go a buster,
I should be lacking in gratitude if I neglected to stuff
you to the brim."

"It is an appointment," affirmed Tricotrin.
"Mind you are not late, for I shall come prepared
to do justice to your hospitality, I promise you!"

And the artist, in high spirits, set forth to investi-
gate the Rue Baba.

He was gratified to discover a café in convenient
proximity to the bureau; and twelve o'clock had not
sounded next day when he took a seat at one of the
little white-topped tables, his gaze bent attentively
upon the agent's step.

For the earliest arrival he had not long to wait.

A dumpy, snub-nosed girl approached, swinging a Ritz bag. She cast a complacent glance at the name on the door, opened the bag, whipped out a powder-puff, and vanished.

"Ciel!" thought the painter. "If she is a fair sample, I have squandered the price of a bock!" He remained in a state of depression for two or three minutes, and then the girl reappeared, evidently in a very bad temper.

"Ho, ho!" he mused, rubbing his hands. "Monsieur Lavelette is plainly a person of his word. No beauty, no engagement! This is going to be all right. Where is the next applicant? I will take another sip to Venus!"

Venus, however, did not irradiate the street yet. The second young woman was too short in the back, and at the sight of her features he shook his head despondently. "No good, my dear," he said to himself. "Little as you suspect it, there is a disappointment for you inside, word of honour! within three minutes I shall behold you again!"

And, sure enough, she made her exit promptly, looking as angry as the other.

"I am becoming a dramatic prophet!" soliloquised Goujaud; "if I had nothing more vital to do, I might win drinks, betting on their chances, with the proprietor of the café. However, I grow impatient for the bevy of beauty—it is a long time on the road!"

As if in obedience to his demand, girls now began to trip into the Rue Baba so rapidly that he was kept busy regarding them. By twos, and threes, and in quartettes they tripped—tall girls, little girls, plain girls, pretty girls, girls shabby, and girls chic. But though many of them would have made agreeable partners at a dance, there was none who possessed the necessary qualifications for The Girl on Satan's Knee. He rolled a cigarette, and blew a pessimistic puff. "Another day lost!" groaned Goujaud. "All is over, I feel it. Posterity will never praise my poster—the clutch of Commerce is upon me—already the smell of the pétrole is in my nostrils!"

And scarcely had he said it when his senses reeled.

For, stepping from a cab, disdainfully, imperially, was his Ideal. Her hair, revealing the lobes of the daintiest ears that ever listened to confessions of love, had the gleam of purple grapes. Her eyes were a mystery, her mouth was a flower, her neck was an intoxication. So violently was the artist affected that, during several moments, he forgot his motive for being there. To be privileged merely to contemplate her was an ecstasy. While he sat transfixed with admiration, her dainty foot graced the agent's step, and she entered.

Goujaud caught his breath, and rose. The cab had been discharged. Dared he speak to her when she came out? It would be a different thing altogether

from speaking to the kind of girl that he had foreseen. But to miss such a model for lack of nerve,
that would be the regret of a lifetime! Now the
prospect of the poster overwhelmed him, and he felt
that he would risk any rebuff, commit any madness
to induce her to "sit."

The estimate that he had, by this time, formed of
Monsieur Lavalette's taste convinced him that her
return would not be yet. He sauntered to and fro,
composing a preliminary and winning phrase. What
was his surprise, after a very few seconds, to see that
she had come out already, and was hastening away!

He overtook her in a dozen strides, and with a
bow that was eloquent of his homage, exclaimed:

"Mademoiselle!"

"Hein?" she said, turning. "Oh, it's all right—
there are too many people there, I've changed my
mind, I shan't wait."

He understood that she took him for a minion of
the agent's, and he hesitated whether to correct her
mistake immediately. However, candour seemed
the better course.

"I do not bring a message from Monsieur Lavalette, mademoiselle," he explained.

"No?"

"No."

"What then?"

"I have ventured to address you on my own account—on a matter of the most urgent importance."

"I have no small change," she said curtly, making to pass.

"Mademoiselle!" His outraged dignity was magnificent. "You mistake me first for an office boy, and then for a beggar. I am a man of means, though my costume may be unconventional. My name is Théodose Goujaud."

Her bow intimated that the name was not significant; but her exquisite eyes had softened at the reference to his means.

"For weeks I have been seeking a face for a picture that I have conceived," he went on; "a face of such peculiar beauty that I despaired of finding it! I had the joy to see you enter the agency, and I waited, trembling with the prayer that I might persuade you to come to my aid. Mademoiselle, will you do me the honour to allow me to reproduce the magic of your features on my canvas? I entreat it of you in the sacred name of Art!"

During this appeal, the lady's demeanour had softened more still. A faint smile hovered on her lips; her gaze was half gratified, half amused.

"Oh, you're an artist?" she said; "you want me to sit to you for the Salon? I don't know, I'm sure."

"It is not precisely for the Salon," he acknowledged. "But I am absorbed by the scheme—it will be the crown of my career. I will explain. It is a long story. If—if we could sit down?"

"Where?"

"There appears to be a café close to the agency," said Goujaud timidly.

"Oh!" She dismissed the café's pretensions with her eyebrows.

"You are right," he stammered. "Now that I look at it again, I see that it is quite a common place. Well, will you permit me to walk a little way with you?"

"We will go to breakfast at Armenonville, if you like," she said graciously, "where you can explain to me at your leisure."

It seemed to Goujaud that his heart dropped into his stomach and turned to a cannon ball there. Armenonville? What would such a breakfast cost? Perhaps a couple of louis! Never in his life had he contemplated breakfasting at Armenonville.

She smiled, as if taking his consent for granted. Her loveliness and air of fashion confused him dreadfully. And if he made excuses, there would be no poster! Oh, he must seize the chance at any price!

"Of course—I shall be enchanted!" he mumbled. And almost before he realised that he was committed to the unprecedented outlay, they were rattling away, side by side in a fiacre.

It was astounding, it was breathless, it was an episode out of a novel! But Goujaud felt too sick, in thinking of the appalling expense, to enjoy his sudden glory. Accustomed to a couple of louis providing meals for three weeks, he was stupefied by the imminence of his "blowing" the sum in a brief half-hour. Even the cab fare weighed upon him; he frequently envied the occupants of omnibuses.

It was clear that the lady herself was no stranger to the restaurant. While he blinked bewildered on the threshold, she was alluding to her "pet table," and calling a waiter "Jules." The menu was a fresh embarrassment to the bohemian, but she, and the deferential waiter, relieved him of that speedily, and in five minutes an epicurean luncheon had been ordered, and he was gulping champagne.

It revived his spirits. Since he had tumbled into the adventure of his life, by all means let him savour the full flavour of it! His companion's smiles had become more frequent, her eyes were more transcendental still.

"How funnily things happen!" she remarked presently, "I had not the least idea of calling on Lavalette when I got up this morning. If I had not had a tiff with somebody, and decided to go on the stage to spite him, I should never have met you."

"Oh, you are not on the stage yet, then?"

"No. But I have often thought about it, and the quarrel determined me. So I jumped into a cab, drove off, and then—well, there was such a crowd of girls there, and they looked so vulgar; I changed my mind."

"Can an angel quarrel?" demanded Goujaud sentimentally. "I cannot imagine you saying an angry word to any one."

"Oh!" she laughed. "Can't I, though! I'm a regular demon when I'm cross. People shouldn't vex me."

"Certainly not," he agreed. "And no one but a brute would do so. Besides, some women are attractive even in a rage. On the whole, I think I should like to see you in a rage with *me,* providing always that you 'made it up' as nicely as I should wish."

"Do you fancy that I could?" she asked, looking at the tablecloth.

"My head swims, in fancying!"

Her laughter rippled again, and her fascination was so intense that the poor fellow could scarcely taste a mouthful of his unique repast. "Talk to me," she commanded, "sensibly I mean! Where do you live?"

"I am living in the Rue Ravignan."

"The Rue Ravignan? Where is that?"

"Montmartre."

"Oh, really." She seemed chilled. "It is not a very nice quarter in the daytime, is it?"

"My studio suits me," murmured Goujaud, perceiving his fall in her esteem. "For that reason I am reluctant to remove. An artist becomes very attached to his studio. And what do I care for fashion, I? You may judge by my coat!"

"You're eccentric, aren't you?"

"Hitherto I have lived only for Art. But now I begin to realise that there may be something more potent and absorbing still."

"What is that?"

"Love!" added Goujaud, feeling himself the embodiment of all the heroes of romance.

"Oh!" Her glance mocked, encouraged. "I am dying to hear about your picture, though! What is the subject?"

"It is not exactly what you mean by a 'picture.'" He fiddled with his glass. "It is, in fact, a poster that I project."

"A poster?" she exclaimed. "And you ask *me* to—oh, no, I couldn't possibly!"

"Mademoiselle!"

"I really don't think I could. A poster? Oh, no!"

"To save me!" he implored. "Because my whole life depends on your decision!"

"How can a poster matter so much to you? The proposal is absurd." She regarded her pêche Melba with a frown.

"If you think of becoming an actress, remember what a splendid advertisement it would be!" he urged feverishly.

"Pouf!" But she had wavered at that.

"All Paris would flock to your début. They would go saying, 'Can she be so beautiful as her portrait?'

And they would come back saying, 'She is lovelier
still!' Let me give you some more wine."

"No more; I'll have coffee, and a grand marnier
—red."

"Doubtless the more expensive colour!" reflected
Goujaud. But the time had passed for dwelling on
minor troubles. "Listen," he resumed; "I shall tell
you my history. You will then realise to what an
abyss of despair your refusal will plunge me—to
what effulgent heights I may be raised by your consent. You cannot be marble! My father——"

"Indeed, I am not marble," she put in. "I am
instinct with sensibility—it is my great weakness."

"So much the better. Be weak to *me*. My
father——"

"Oh, let us get out of this first!" she suggested.
"You can talk to me as we drive."

And the attentive Jules presented the discreetly
folded bill.

For fully thirty seconds Armenonville swirled
round the unfortunate painter so violently that his
faculties failed him. He feared that the siren must
hear the pounding of his heart. To think that he had
dreaded paying two louis! Two louis, why, it would
have been a bagatelle! Speechlessly he laid a fortune
on the salver. With a culminating burst of recklessness he waved four francs towards Jules, and remarked that that personage eyed the tip with cold
displeasure. "What a lucrative career, a waiter's!"

moaned the artist; "he turns up his nose at four francs!"

Well, he had speculated too heavily to accept defeat now! Bracing himself for the effort, Goujaud besought the lady's help with such a flood of blandishment during the drive that more than once she seemed at the point of yielding. Only a difficult detail had he withheld—that he wished to pose her on the knee of Mephistopheles—and to propitiate her further, before breaking the news, he stopped the cab at a florist's.

She was so good humoured and tractable after the florist had pillaged him that he could scarcely be callous when she showed him that she had split her glove. But, to this day, he protests that, until the glove shop had been entered, it never occurred to him that it would be necessary to present her with more than one pair. As they came out—Goujaud moving beside her like a man in a trance—she gave a faint start.

"Mon Dieu!" she muttered. "There's my friend —he has seen us—I must speak to him, or he will think I am doing wrong. Wait a minute!" And a dandy, with a monocle, was, indeed, casting very supercilious glances at the painter.

At eight o'clock that evening, M. Tricotrin, with a prodigious appetite, sat in the Faisan d'Or, awaiting the arrival of his host. When impatience was mastering him, there arrived, instead, a petit bleu.

The impecunious poet took it from the proprietress, paling, and read:

"I discovered my Ideal—she ruined, and then deserted me. To-morrow there will be an artist the less, and a pétrole-merchant the more. Pardon my non-appearance—I am spending my last sous on this message."

"Monsieur will give his order now?" inquired Madame.

"Er—thank you, I do not dine to-night," said Tricotrin.

XI

"PARDON, YOU ARE MADEMOISELLE GIRARD!"

A NEWSVENDOR passed along the terrace of the Café d'Harcourt bawling "La Voix Parisienne." The Frenchman at my table made a gesture of aversion. Our eyes met; I said:

"You do not like 'La Voix'?"

He answered with intensity:

"I loathe it."

"What's its offence?"

The wastrel frowned; he fiddled with his frayed and filthy collar.

"You revive painful associations; you ask me for a humiliating story," he murmured—and regarded his empty glass.

I can take a hint as well as most people.

He prepared his poison reflectively.

"I will tell you all!" he said.

One autumn the editor of "La Voix" announced to the assistant-editor: "I have a great idea for booming the paper!"

The assistant-editor gazed at him respectfully.

"I propose to prove, in the public interest, the difficulty of tracing a missing person. I shall instruct a member of the staff to disappear. I shall publish his description and his portrait. And I shall offer a prize to the first stranger who identifies him."

The assistant-editor had tact, and he did not reply that the idea had already been worked in London with a disappearing lady. He replied:

"What an original scheme!"

"It might be even more effective that the disappearing person should be a lady," added the chief, like one inspired.

"That," cried the assistant-editor, "is the top brick of genius!"

So the editor reviewed the brief list of his lady contributors, and sent for Mademoiselle Girard.

His choice fell upon Mademoiselle Girard for two reasons. First, she was not facially remarkable—a smudgy woodcut of her would look much like a smudgy woodcut of anybody else. Second, she was not widely known in Paris, being at the beginning of her career; in fact, she was so inexperienced that hitherto she had been entrusted only with criticism.

However, the young woman had all her buttons on; and after he had talked to her, she said cheerfully:

"Without a chaperon I should be conspicuous, and without a fat purse I should be handicapped. So is understood that I am to provide myself with a suitable companion, and to draw upon the office for expenses?"

"Mademoiselle," returned the editor, "the purpose of the paper is to portray a drama of life, not to emulate an opéra bouffe. I shall explain more fully. Please figure to yourself that you are a young girl in an unhappy home. Let us suppose that a stepmother is at fault. You feel that you can submit to her oppression no longer; you resolve to be free, or to end your troubles in the Seine. Weeping, you pack your modest handbag; you cast a last lingering look at the oil painting of your own dear mother, who is with the angels in the drawing-room; that is to say, of your own dear mother in the drawing-room, who is with the angels. (It still hangs there; your father has insisted on it.) Unheard, you steal from the house; the mysterious city of Paris stretches before your friendless feet. Can you engage a chaperon? Can you draw upon an office for expenses? The idea is laughable. You have saved, at a liberal computation, fifty francs; it is necessary for you to find employment without delay. But what happens? Your father is distracted by your loss; the thought of the perils that beset you frenzies him; he invokes the aid of the police. Well, the object of our experiment is to demonstrate that, in spite of an advertised reward, in spite of a published portrait, in spite of the public's zeal itself, you will be passed on the Boulevards and in the slums by myriads of unsuspecting eyes for weeks."

The girl inquired, much less blithely:

"How long is this experiment to continue?"

"It will continue until you are identified, of course. The longer the period, the more triumphant our demonstration."

"And I am to have no more than fifty francs to exist on all the time? Monsieur, the job does not call to me."

"You are young and you fail to grasp the value of your opportunity," said the editor, with paternal tolerance. "From such an assignment you will derive experiences that will be of the highest benefit to your future. Rejoice, my child! Very soon I shall give you final instructions."

The Frenchman lifted his glass, which was again empty.

"I trust my voice does not begin to grate upon you?" he asked solicitously. "Much talking affects my uvula."

I made a trite inquiry.

He answered that, since I was so pressing, he would!

"Listen!" he resumed, after a sip.

I am not in a position to say whether the young lady humoured the editor by rejoicing, but she obeyed him by going forth. Her portrait was duly

published, "La Voix" professed ignorance of her
whereabouts from the moment that she left the Rue
Louis-le-Grand, and a prize of two thousand francs
was to reward the first stranger who said to her,
"Pardon, you are Mademoiselle Girard!" In every
issue the Public were urged towards more strenuous
efforts to discover her, and all Paris bought the
paper, with amusement, to learn if she was found
yet.

At the beginning of the week, misgivings were
ingeniously hinted as to her fate. On the tenth day
the editor printed a letter (which he had written
himself), hotly condemning him for exposing a poor
girl to danger. It was signed "An Indignant
Parent," and teemed with the most stimulating suggestions. Copies of "La Voix" were as popular as
peanuts at a fair. When a fortnight had passed, the
prize was increased to three thousand francs, and
many young men resigned less promising occupa-
tions, such as authorship and the fine arts, in order
to devote themselves exclusively to the search.

Personally, I had something else to do. I am an
author (as you may have divined by the rhythm of
my impromptu phrases); but it happened at that time
that a play of mine had been accepted by the Grand-
Guignol, subject to an additional thrill being introduced, and I preferred pondering for a thrill in my
garret to hunting for a pin in a haystack.

Enfin, I completed the drama to the Management's satisfaction, and received a comely little cheque in payment. It was the first cheque that I had seen for years! I embraced myself; I paid to be shaved; I committed no end of follies.

How good is life when one is rich—immediately one joins the optimists! I feared the future no longer; I was hungry, and I let my appetite do as it liked with me. I lodged in Montmartre, and it was my custom to eat at the unpretentious Faisan d'Or, when I ate at all; but that morning my mood demanded something resplendent. Rumours had reached me of a certain Café Éclatant, where for one-franc-fifty one might breakfast on five epicurean courses amid palms and plush. I said I would go the pace. I adventured the Café Éclatant.

The interior realised my most sanguine expectations. The room would have done no discredit to the Grands Boulevards. I was so much exhilarated that I ordered a half bottle of barsac, though I noted that here it cost ten sous more than at the Faisan, and I prepared to enjoy the unwonted extravagance of my repast to the concluding crumb.

Monsieur, there are events in life of which it is difficult to speak without bitterness. When I recall the disappointment of that déjeûner at the Café Éclatant, my heart swells with rage. The soup was slush, the fish tasted like washing, the meat was rags. "Dessert" consisted of wizened grapes; the one thing fit to eat was the cheese.

As I meditated on the sum that I had squandered, I could have cried with mortification, and, to make matters more pathetic still, I was as hungry as ever. I sat seeking some caustic epigram to wither the dame-de-comptoir, and presently the door opened and another victim entered. Her face was pale and interesting. I saw, by her hesitation, that the place was strange to her. An accomplice of the chief brigand pounced on her immediately, and bore her to a table opposite. The misguided girl was about to waste one-franc-fifty. I felt that I owed a duty to her in this crisis. The moment called for instant action; before she could decide between slush and hors d'œuvres, I pulled an envelope from my pocket, scribbled a warning, and expressed it to her by the robber who had brought my bill.

I had written, "The déjeûner is dreadful. Escape!"

It reached her in the nick of time. She read the wrong side of the envelope first, and was evidently puzzled. Then she turned it over. A look of surprise, a look of thankfulness, rendered her still more fascinating. I perceived that she was inventing an excuse—that she pretended to have forgotten something. She rose hastily and went out. My barsac was finished—shocking bad tipple it was for the money—and now I, too, got up and left. When I issued into the street, I found her waiting for me.

"I think you are the knight to whom gratitude is due, monsieur?" she murmured graciously.

"Mademoiselle," I responded, "you magnify the importance of my service."

"It was a gallant deed," she insisted. "You have saved me from a great misfortune—perhaps greater than you understand. My finances are at their lowest ebb, and to have beggared myself for an impossible meal would have been no joke. Thanks to you, I may still breakfast satisfactorily somewhere else. Is it treating you like Baedeker's Guide to the Continent if I ask you to recommend a restaurant?"

"Upon my word, I doubt if you can do better than the Faisan d'Or," I said. "A moment ago I was lacerated with regret that I had not gone there. But there is a silver lining to every hash-house, and my choice of the Éclatant has procured me the glory of your greeting."

She averted her gaze with a faint smile. She had certainly charm. Admiration and hunger prompted me to further recklessness. I said: "This five-course swindle has left me ravenous, and I am bound for the Faisan myself. May I beg for the rapture of your company there?"

"Monsieur, you overwhelm me with chivalries," she replied; "I shall be enchanted." And, five minutes later, the Incognita and I were polishing off smoked herring and potato salad, like people who had no time to lose.

"Do you generally come here?" she asked, when we had leisure.

"Infrequently—no oftener than I have a franc in my pocket. But details of my fasts would form a poor recital, and I make a capital listener."

"You also make a capital luncheon," she remarked.

"Do not prevaricate," I said severely. "I am consumed with impatience to hear the history of your life. Be merciful and communicative."

"Well, I am young, fair, accomplished, and of an amiable disposition," she began, leaning her elbows on the table.

"These things are obvious. Come to confidences! What is your profession?"

"By profession I am a clairvoyante and palmist," she announced.

I gave her my hand at once, and I was in two minds about giving her my heart. "Proceed," I told her; "reveal my destiny!"

Her air was profoundly mystical.

"In the days of your youth," she proclaimed, "your line of authorship is crossed by many rejections."

"Oho, I am an author, am I? That's a fine thing in guesses!"

"It is written!" she affirmed, still scrutinising my palm. "Your dramatic lines are—er—countless; some of them are good. I see danger; you should beware of—I cannot distinguish!" she clasped her brow and shivered. "Ah, I have it! You should beware of hackneyed situations."

"So the Drama is 'written,' too, is it?"

"It is written, and I discern that it is already accepted," she said. "For at the juncture where the Café Éclatant is eclipsed by the Restaurant du Faisan d'Or, there is a distinct manifestation of cash."

"Marvellous!" I exclaimed. "And can the sibyl explain why she surmised that I was a dramatic author?"

"Even so!" she boasted. "You wrote your message to me on an envelope from the Dramatic Authors' Society. What do you think of my palmistry?"

"I think so little of it, that I am quite sure it is not your career. You are more likely an author, yourself, or an actress, or a journalist. Perhaps you are Mademoiselle Girard. Mon Dieu! What a piece of luck for me if I found Mademoiselle Girard!"

"And what a piece of luck for her!"

"Why for her?"

"Well, she cannot be having a rollicking time. It would not break her heart to be found, one may be certain."

"In that case," I said, "she has only to give some-one the tip."

"Oh, that would be dishonourable—she has a duty to fulfil to 'La Voix,' she must wait till she is identi-

fied. And, remember, there must be no half measures
—the young man must have the intuition to say
firmly, 'Pardon, you are Mademoiselle Girard!' "

Her earnest gaze met mine for an instant.

"As a matter of fact," I said, "I do not see how
anyone can be expected to identify her in the street.
The portrait shows her without a hat, and a hat
makes a tremendous difference."

She sighed.

"What is your trouble?" I asked.

"Man!"

"Man? Tell me his address, that I may slay
him."

"The whole sex! Its impenetrable stupidity. If
Mademoiselle Girard is ever recognised it will be by
a woman. Man has no instinct."

"May one inquire the cause of these flattering
reflections?"

Her laughter pealed.

"Let us talk of something else!" she commanded.
"When does your play come out, Monsieur Thibaud
Hippolyte Duboc? You see I learnt your name,
too?"

"You have all the advantages," I complained.
"Will you take a second cup of coffee, Mademoiselle
—er——?"

"No, thank you, monsieur," she said.

"Will you take a liqueur, Mademoiselle—
er——?"

"Mademoiselle Er will not take a liqueur either," she pouted.

"Well, will you take a walk?"

We sauntered to the Buttes-Chaumont, and very agreeable I found it there. We chose a seat in the shade, and I began to feel that I had known her all my life. More precisely, perhaps, I began to feel that I wished to know her all my life. A little breeze was whispering through the boughs, and she lifted her face to it gratefully.

"How delicious," she said. "I should like to take off my hat!"

"Do then!"

"Shall I?"

"Why not?"

She pulled the pins out slowly, and laid the hat aside, and raised her eyes to me, smiling.

"Well?" she murmured.

"You are beautiful!"

"Is that all?"

"What more would you have me say?"

The glare of sunshine mellowed while we talked; clocks struck unheeded by me. It amazed me at last, to discover how long she had held me captive. Still, I knew nothing of her affairs, excepting that she was hard up—that, by comparison, I was temporarily prosperous. I did not even know where she meant to go when we moved, nor did it appear necessary to inquire yet, for the sentiment in her tones assured me that she would dismiss me with no heartless haste.

Two men came strolling past the bench, and one of them stared at her so impudently that I burned with indignation. After looking duels at him, I turned to her, to deprecate his rudeness. Judge of my dismay when I perceived that she was shuddering with emotion! Jealousy blackened the gardens to me.

"Who is that man?" I exclaimed.

"I don't know," she faltered.

"You don't know? But you are trembling?"

"Am I?"

"I ask you who he is? How he dared to look at you like that?"

"Am I responsible for the way a loafer looks?"

"You are responsible for your agitation; I ask you to explain it!"

"And by what right, after all?"

"By what right? Wretched, false-hearted girl! Has our communion for hours given me no rights? Am I a Frenchman, or a flounder? Answer; you are condemning me to tortures! Why did you tremble under that man's eyes?"

"I was afraid," she stammered.

"Afraid?"

"Afraid that he had recognised me."

"Mon Dieu! Of what are you guilty?"

"I am not guilty."

"Of what are you accused?"

"I can tell you nothing," she gasped.

"You shall tell me all!" I swore. "In the name of my love I demand it of you. Speak! Why did you fear his recognition?"

Her head drooped pitifully;

"Because I wanted *you* to recognise me first!"

For a tense moment I gazed at her bewildered. In the next, I cursed myself for a fool—I blushed for my suspicions, my obtuseness—I sought dizzily the words, the prescribed words that I must speak;

"Pardon," I shouted, "you are Mademoiselle Girard!"

She sobbed:

"What have I done?"

"You have done a great and generous thing! I am humbled before you! I bless you! I don't know how I could have been such a dolt as not to guess!"

"Oh, how I wish you had guessed! You have been so kind to me, I longed for you to guess! And now I have betrayed a trust. I have been a bad journalist."

"You have been a good friend. Courage! No one will ever hear what has happened. And, anyhow, it is all the same to the paper whether the prize is paid to me or to somebody else."

"Yes," she admitted. "That is true. Oh, when that man turned round and looked at me, I thought your chance had gone! I made sure it was all over! Well"—she forced a smile—"it is no use my being sorry, is it? Mademoiselle Girard is 'found'!"

"But you must not be sorry," I said. "Come, a disagreeable job is finished! And you have the additional satisfaction of knowing the money goes to a fellow you don't altogether dislike. What do I have to do about it, hein?"

"You must telegraph to 'La Voix' at once that you have identified me. Then, in the morning you should go to the office. I can depend upon you, can't I? You will never give me away to a living soul?"

"Word of honour!" I vowed. "What do you take me for? Do tell me you don't regret! There's a dear! Tell me you don't regret!"

She threw back her head dauntlessly.

"No," she said, "I don't regret. Only, in justice to me, remember that I was treacherous in order to do a turn to you, not to escape my own discomforts. To be candid, I believe I wish that we had met in two or three weeks' time, instead of to-day!"

"Why that?"

"In two or three weeks' time the prize was to be raised to five thousand francs, to keep up the excitement."

"Ciel!" I cried. "Five thousand francs! Do you know that positively?"

"Oh, yes!" She nodded. "It is arranged."

Five thousand francs would have been a fortune to me.

Neither of us spoke for some seconds. Then continuing my thoughts aloud, I said:

"After all why should I telegraph at once? What is to prevent my waiting the two or three weeks?"

"Oh, to allow you to do that would be scandalous of me," she demurred; "I should be actually swindling 'La Voix'!"

" 'La Voix' will obtain a magnificent advertisement for its outlay, which is all that it desires," I argued; "the boom will be worth five thousand francs to 'La Voix,' there is no question of swindling. Five thousand francs is a sum with which one might——"

"It can't be done," she persisted.

"To a man in my position," I said, "five thousand francs——"

"It is impossible for another reason! As I told you, I am at the end of my resources. I rose this morning, praying that I should be identified. My landlady has turned me out, and I have no more than the price of one meal to go on with."

"You goose!" I laughed. "And if I were going to net five thousand francs by your tip three weeks hence, don't you suppose it would be good enough for me to pay your expenses in the meanwhile?"

She was silent again. I understood that her conscience was a more formidable drawback than her penury.

Monsieur, I said that you had asked me for a humiliating story—that I had poignant memories connected with "La Voix." Here is one of them:

I set myself to override her scruples—to render this girl false to her employers!

Many men might have done so without remorse. But not a man like me. I am naturally high-minded, of the most sensitive honour. Even when I conquered at last, I could not triumph. Far from it! I blamed the force of circumstances furiously for compelling me to sacrifice my principles to my purse. Hein? I am no adventurer.

Enfin, the problem now was, where was I to hide her? Her portmanteau she had deposited at a railway station. Should we have it removed to another bedroom, or to a pension de famille? Both plans were open to objections—a bedroom would necessitate her still challenging discovery in restaurants; and at a pension, she would run risks on the premises. A pretty kettle of fish if someone spotted her while I was holding for the rise!

We debated the point exhaustively. And, having yielded, she displayed keen intelligence in arranging for the best. Finally she declared:

"Of the two things, a pension is to be preferred. Instal me there as your sister! Remember that people picture me a wanderer and alone; therefore, a lady who is introduced by her brother, is in

small danger of being recognised as Mademoiselle
Girard."

She was right, I perceived it. We found an excellent pension, where I was unknown. I presented
her as "Mademoiselle Henriette Delafosse, my
sister." And, to be on the safe side, I engaged a
private sitting-room for her, explaining that she was
somewhat neurasthenic.

Good! I waited breathless now for every edition
of "La Voix," thinking that her price might advance
even sooner. But she closed at three thousand francs
daily. Girard stood firm, but there was no upward
tendency. Every afternoon I called on her. She
talked about that conscience of hers again sometimes, and it did not prove quite so delightful as I
had expected, when I paid a visit. Especially when
I paid a bill as well.

Monsieur, my disposition is most liberal. But
when I had been mulcted in the second bill, I confess
that I became a trifle downcast. I had prepared myself to nourish the girl wholesomely, as befitted the
circumstances, but I had said nothing of vin supérieur
and I noted that she had been asking for it as if
it were cider in Normandy. The list of extras in
those bills gave me the jumps, and the charges
made for scented soap were nothing short of an
outrage.

Well, there was but one more week to bear now,
and during the week I allowed her to revel. This,

though I was approaching embarrassments *re* the rent of my own attic!

How strange is life! Who shall foretell the future? I had wrestled with my self-respect, I had nursed an investment which promised stupendous profits were I capable of carrying my scheme to a callous conclusion. But could I do it? Did I claim the prize, which had already cost me so much? Monsieur, you are a man of the world, a judge of character: I ask you, did I claim the prize, or did I not?"

He threw himself back in the chair, and toyed significantly with his empty glass.

I regarded him, his irresolute mouth, his receding chin, his unquenchable thirst for absinthe. I regarded him and I paid him no compliments. I said:

"You claimed the prize."

"You have made a bloomer," he answered. "I did not claim it. The prize was claimed by the wife of a piano-tuner, who had discovered Mademoiselle Girard employed in the artificial flower department of the Printemps. I read the blood-curdling news at nine o'clock on a Friday evening; and at 9.15, when I hurled myself, panic-stricken, into the pension, the impostor who had tricked me out of three weeks' board and lodging had already done a bolt. I have never had the joy of meeting her since."

XII

THE LAST EFFECT

JEAN BOURJAC was old and lazy. Why should he work any more? In his little cottage he was content enough. If the place was not precisely gay, could he not reach Paris for a trifle? And if he had no neighbours to chat with across the wall, weren't there his flowers to tend in the garden? Occasionally— because one cannot shake off the interests of a life-time—he indulged in an evening at the Folies-Bergère, or Olympia, curious to witness some Illusion that had made a hit.

At such times old Bourjac would chuckle and wag his head sagely, for he saw no Illusions now to compare with those invented by himself when he was in the business.

And there were many persons who admitted that he had been supreme in his line. At the Folies-Bergère he was often recognised and addressed as "Maître."

One summer evening, when old Bourjac sat reading *Le Journal,* Margot, the housekeeper, who had grown deaf and ancient in his service, announced a stranger. She was a girl with a delicate oval face, and the kind of eyes one associates with Angels.

"Monsieur Bourjac," she began, as if reciting a speech that she had studied, "I have come out here to beg a favour of you. I thirst for a career behind the footlights. Alas! I cannot sing, or dance, or act. There is only one chance for me—to possess an Illusion that shall take Paris by storm. I am told that there is nothing produced to-day fit to hold a candle to the former 'Miracles Bourjac.' Will you help me? Will you design for me the most wonderful Illusion of your life?"

"Mademoiselle," said Bourjac, with a shrug, "I have retired."

"I implore you!" she urged. "But I have not finished; I am poor, I am employed at a milliner's, I could not pay down a single franc. My offer is a share of my salary as a star. I am mad for the stage. It is not the money that I crave for, but the applause. I would not grudge you even half my salary! Oh! Monsieur, it is in your power to lift me from despair into paradise. Say you consent."

Bourjac mused. Her offer was very funny; if she had been of the ordinary type, he would have sent her packing, with a few commercial home truths. Excitement had brought a flush to the oval face, her glorious eyes awoke in him emotions which he had believed extinct. She was so captivating that he cast about him for phrases to prolong the interview.

Though he could not agree, he didn't want her to go yet.

And when she did rise at last, he murmured: "Well, well, see me again and we will talk about it. I have no wish to be hard, you understand."

Her name was Laure. She was in love with a conjurer, a common, flashy fellow, who gave his mediocre exhibitions of legerdemain at such places as Le Jardin Extérieur, and had recently come to lodge at her mother's. She aspired to marry him, but did not dare to expect it. Her homage was very palpable, and M. Eugène Legrand, who had no matrimonial intentions, would often wish that the old woman did not keep such a sharp eye upon her.

Needless to say, Bourjac's semi-promise sent her home enraptured. She had gone to him on impulse, without giving her courage time to take flight; now, in looking back, she wondered at her audacity, and that she had gained so much as she had. "I have no wish to be hard," he had said. Oh, the old rascal admired her hugely! If she coaxed enough, he would end by giving in. What thumping luck! She determined to call upon him again on Sunday, and to look her best.

Bourjac, however, did not succumb on Sunday. Fascinating as he found her, he squirmed at the prospect of the task demanded of him. His workshop in the garden had been closed so long that rats had begun to regard it as their playroom; the more he contemplated resuming his profession the less inclined he felt to do it.

She paid him many visits and he became deeply infatuated with her, yet he continued to maintain that he was past such an undertaking—that she had applied to him too late.

Then, one day, after she had flown into a passion, and wept, and been mollified, he said hesitatingly:—

"I confess that an idea for an Illusion has occurred to me, but I do not pledge myself to execute it. I should call it 'A Life.' An empty cabinet is examined; it is supported by four columns—there is no stage trap, no obscurity, no black velvet curtain concealed in the dark, to screen the operations; the cabinet is raised high above the ground, and the lights are full up. You understand?" Some of the inventor's enthusiasm had crept into his voice. "You understand?"

"Go on," she said, holding her breath.

"Listen! The door of the cabinet is slammed, and in letters of fire there appears on it, 'Scene I.' Instantaneously it flies open again and discloses a baby. The baby moves, it wails—in fine, it is alive. Slam! Letters of fire, 'Scene II.' Instantaneously the baby has vanished; in its place is a beautiful girl —you! You smile triumphantly at your reflection in a mirror; your path is strewn with roses, the world is at your feet. Slam! 'Scene III.' In a moment twenty years have passed; your hair is grey, you are matronly, stout, your face is no longer oval; yet unmistakably it is you yourself, the same woman. Slam! 'Scene IV.' You are enfeebled, a crone, toothless, tottering on a stick. Once more! It is the last effect—the door flies open and reveals a skeleton."

"You can make this?" she questioned.

"I could make it if I chose," he answered.

"Will you?"

"It depends."

"On what?"

"On you!"

"Take any share you want," she cried, "I will sign anything you like! After all, would not the success be due to you?"

"So you begin to see that?" said the old man dryly. "But, I repeat, it depends! In spite of everything, you may think my terms too high."

"What do you want me to do?" she stammered.

"Marry me!" said Bourjac.

He did not inquire if she had any affection for him; he knew that if she said "Yes" it would be a lie. But he adored this girl, who, of a truth, had nothing but her beauty to recommend her, and he persuaded himself that his devotion would evoke tenderness in her by degrees. She found the price high indeed. Not only was she young enough to be his grand-daughter, but she had given her fancy to another man. Immediately, she could not consent. When

she took leave of him, it was understood that she
would think the offer over; and she went home and
let Legrand hear that Bourjac had proposed for her
hand. If, by any chance, the news piqued Legrand
into doing likewise——?

But Legrand said nothing to the point. Though
he was a little chagrined by the intelligence, it never
even entered his mind to attempt to cut the inventor
out. How should it? She was certainly an attractive girl, but as to marrying her—— He thought
Bourjac a fool! As for himself, if he married at all,
it would be an artist who was drawing a big salary,
and who would be able to provide him with some of
the good things of life. "I pray you will be very
happy, mademoiselle," he said, putting on a sentimental air.

So, after she had cried with mortification, Laure
promised to be old Bourjac's wife.

A few weeks later they were married, and in that
lonely little cottage she would have been bored to
death but for the tawdry future that she foresaw.
The man's dream of awaking her tenderness was
speedily dispelled; he had been accepted as the means
to an end, and he was held fast to the compact. She
grudged him every hour in which he idled by her
side. Driven from her arms by her impatience, old
Bourjac would toil patiently in the workroom—
planning, failing, surmounting obstacles inch by
inch, for the sake of a woman whose sole interest in

his existence was his progress with the Illusion that was to gratify her vanity.

He worshipped her still. If he had not worshipped her, he would more than once have renounced the scheme as impracticable; only his love for her supported him in the teeth of the impediments that arose. Of these she heard nothing. For one reason, her interest was so purely selfish that she had not even wished to learn how the cabinet was to be constructed; "All those figures gave her a headache," she declared. For another, when early in the winter he had owned himself at a deadlock, she had sneered at him as a duffer who was unable to fulfil his boasts. Old Bourjac never forgot that—his reputation was very dear to him—he did not speak to her of his difficulties again.

But they often talked of the success she was to achieve. She liked to go into a corner of the parlour and rehearse the entrance that she would make to acknowledge the applause. "It will be the great moment," she would say, "when I re-appear as myself and bow."

"No, it will be expected; that will not surprise anybody," Bourjac would insist. "The climax, the last effect, will be the skeleton!"

It was the skeleton that caused him the most anxious thought of all. In order to compass it, he almost feared that he would be compelled to sacrifice one of the preceding scenes. The babe, the girl, the matron, the crone, for all these his mechanism provided; but the skeleton, the "last effect," baffled his ingenuity. Laure began to think his task eternal.

Ever since the wedding, she had dilated proudly to her mother and Legrand on her approaching début, and it angered her that she could never say when the début was to be. Now that there need be no question of his marrying her, Legrand's manner towards her had become more marked. She went to the house often. One afternoon, when she rang, the door was opened by him; he explained that the old woman was out marketing.

Laure waited in the kitchen, and the conjurer sat on the table, talking to her.

"How goes the Illusion?" he asked.

"Oh, big!" she said. "It's going to knock them, I can tell you!" Her laugh was rather derisive. "It's a rum world. The shop-girl will become an artist, with a show that draws all Paris! We expect to open at the Folies-Bergère." She knew that Legrand could never aspire to an engagement at the Folies-Bergère as long as he lived.

"I hope you will make a hit," he said, understanding her resentment perfectly.

"You did not foresee me a star turn, hein?"

He gave a shrug. "How could I foresee? If you had not married Bourjac, of course it would not have happened?"

"I suppose not," she murmured. She was sorry

he realised that; she would have liked him to feel that she might have had the Illusion anyhow, and been a woman worth his winning.

"Indeed," added Legrand pensively, rolling a cigarette, "you have done a great deal to obtain a success. It is not every girl who would go to such lengths."

"What?" She coloured indignantly.

"I mean it is not every girl who would break the heart of a man who loved her."

They looked in each other's eyes for a moment. Then she turned her head scornfully away.

"Why do you talk rot to me? Do you take me for a kid?"

He decided that a pained silence would be most effective.

"If you cared about me, why didn't you say so?" she flashed, putting the very question he had hoped for.

"Because my position prevented it," he sighed. "I could not propose, a poor devil like me! Do I lodge in an attic from choice? But you are the only woman I ever wanted for my wife."

After a pause, she said softly, "I never knew you cared."

"I shall never care for anybody else," he answered. And then her mother came in with the vegetables.

It is easy to believe what one wishes, and she wished to believe Legrand's protestations. She began to pity herself profoundly, feeling that she had thrown away the substance for the shadow. In the sentimentality to which she yielded, even the prospect of being a "star turn" failed to console her, and during the next few weeks she invented reasons for visiting at her mother's more frequently than ever.

After these visits, Legrand used to smirk to himself in his attic. He reflected that the "turn" would, probably, earn a substantial salary for a long time to come. If he persuaded her to run away with him when the show had been produced, it would be no bad stroke of business for him! Accordingly, in their conversations, he advised her to insist on the Illusion being her absolute property.

"One can never tell what can occur," he would say. "If the managers arranged with Bourjac, not with you, you would always be dependent on your husband's whims for your engagements." And, affecting unconsciousness of his real meaning, the woman would reply, "That's true; yes, I suppose it would be best—yes, I shall have all the engagements made with *me*."

But by degrees even such pretences were dropped between them; they spoke plainly. He had the audacity to declare that it tortured him to think of her in old Bourjac's house—old Bourjac who plodded all day to minister to her caprice! She, no less shameless, acknowledged that her loneliness there was almost unendurable. So Legrand used to call upon her, to cheer her solitude, and while Bourjac laboured in the workroom, the lovers lolled in the parlour, and talked of the future they would enjoy together when his job was done.

"See, monsieur—your luncheon!" mumbled Margot, carrying a tray into the workroom on his busiest days.

"And Madame, has Madame her luncheon?" shouted Bourjac. Margot was very deaf indeed.

"Madame entertains Monsieur Legrand again," returned the housekeeper, who was not blind as well.

Bourjac understood the hint, and more than once he remonstrated with his wife. But she looked in his eyes and laughed suspicion out of him for the time: "Eugène was an old friend, whom she had known from childhood! Enfin, if Jean objected, she would certainly tell him not to come so often. It was very ridiculous, however!"

And afterwards she said to Legrand, "We must put up with him in the meanwhile; be patient, darling! We shall not have to worry about what he thinks much longer!"

Then, as if to incense her more, Bourjac was attacked by rheumatism before the winter finished; he could move only with the greatest difficulty, and had to take to his bed. Day after day he lay there, and she fumed at the sight of him, passive under the blankets, while his work was at a standstill.

More than ever the dulness got on her nerves now, especially as since the complaint about the frequency of his visits, Legrand had avoided the house alto-gether. He was about to leave Paris to fulfil some engagements in the provinces. It occurred to her that it would be a delightful change to accompany him for a week. She had formerly had an aunt living in Rouen, and she told Bourjac that she had been invited to stay with her for a few days.

Bourjac made no objection. Only, as she hummed gaily over her packing, he turned his old face to the wall to hide his tears.

Her luggage was dispatched in advance, and by Legrand's counsel, it was labelled at the last minute with an assumed name. If he could have done so without appearing indifferent to her society, Legrand would have dissuaded her from indulging in the trip, for he had resolved now to be most circumspect until the Illusion was inalienably her own. As it was, he took all the precautions possible. They would travel separately; he was to depart in the evening, and Laure would follow by the next train. When she arrived, he would be awaiting her.

With the removal of her trunk, her spirits rose higher still. But the day passed slowly. At dusk she sauntered about the sitting-room, wishing that it were time for her to start. She had not seen Le-grand since the previous afternoon, when they had met at a café to settle the final details. When the clock struck again, she reckoned that he must be nearly at his destination; perhaps he was there already, pacing the room as she paced this one? She laughed. Not a tinge of remorse discoloured the pleasure of her outlook—her adieu to her husband was quite careless. The average woman who sins longs to tear out her conscience for marring moments which would otherwise be perfect. This woman had absolutely no conscience.

The shortest route to the station was by the garden gate; as she raised the latch, she was amazed to see Legrand hurriedly approaching.

"Thank goodness, I have caught you!" he exclaimed. "I nearly went round to the front!"

"What has happened?"

"Nothing serious; I am not going, that is all— they have changed my date. The matter has been uncertain all day, or I would have let you know earlier. It is lucky I was in time to prevent your starting!"

She was dumb with disappointment.

"It is a nuisance about your luggage," he went on. "We must telegraph about it. Don't look so down in the mouth—we shall have our trip next week instead."

"What am I to say to Jean—he will think it so strange? I have said 'Good-bye' to him."

"Oh, you can find an excuse—you 'missed your train.' Come out for half an hour, and we can talk."

His glance fell on the workroom. "Is that fastened up?"

"I don't know. Do you want to see what he has done?"

"I may as well!" He had never had an opportunity before—Bourjac had always been in there.

"No, it isn't locked," she said; "come on then! Wait till I have shut it after us before you strike a match—Margot might see the light."

A rat darted across their feet as they lit the lamp, and he dropped the matchbox. "Ugh!"

"The beastly things!" she shivered. "Make haste!"

On the floor stood a cabinet that was not unlike a gloomy wardrobe in its outward aspect. Legrand examined it curiously.

"Too massive!" he remarked. "It will cost a fortune for carriage—and where are the columns I heard of?" He stepped inside and sounded the walls. "Humph, of course I see his idea, the fake is a very old one, but it is always effective." Really, he knew nothing about it, but as he was a conjurer, she accepted him as an authority.

"Show me! Is there room for us both?" she said, getting in after him. And as she got in, the door slammed.

Instantaneously they were in impenetrable darkness, jammed close together. Their four hands flew all over the door at once, but they could touch no handle. The next moment, some revolving apparatus that had been set in motion, flung them off their feet. Round and round it swirled, striking against their bodies and their faces. They grovelled to escape it, but their efforts were futile in the darkness; they could not even see its shape.

"Stop it!" she gasped.

"I don't know how," he panted.

After a few seconds the whir grew fainter, the gyrations stopped automatically. She wiped the blood from her face, and burst into hysterical weeping. The man, cursing horribly, rapped to find the spring that she must have pressed as she entered. It seemed to them both that there could be no spot he did not rap a thousand times, but the door never budged.

His curses ceased; he crouched by her, snorting with fear.

"What shall we do?" she muttered.

He did not answer her.

"Eugène, let us stamp! Perhaps the spring is in the floor."

Still he paid no heed—he was husbanding his breath. When a minute had passed, she felt his chest distend, and a scream broke from him—*"Help!"*

"Mon Dieu!" She clutched him, panic-stricken. "We mustn't be found here, it would ruin everything. Feel for the spring! Eugène, feel for the spring, don't call!"

"Help!"

"Don't you understand? Jean will guess—it will be the end of my hopes, I shall have no career!"

"I have myself to think about!" he whimpered. And pushing away her arms, he screamed again and again. But there was no one to hear him, no neighbours, no one passing in the fields—none but old Bourjac, and deaf Margot, beyond earshot, in the house.

The cabinet was, of course, ventilated, and the danger was, not suffocation, but that they would be jammed here while they slowly starved to death. Soon her terror of the fate grew all-powerful in the woman, and, though she loathed him for having been the first to call, she, too, shrieked constantly for help now. By turns, Legrand would yell, distraught, and heave himself helplessly against the door—they were so huddled that he could bring no force to bear upon it.

In their black, pent prison, like a coffin on end, the night held a hundred hours. The matchbox lay outside, where it had fallen, and though they could hear his watch ticking in his pocket, they were unable to look at it. After the watch stopped, they lost their sense of time altogether; they disputed what day of the week it was.

Their voices had been worn to whispers now; they croaked for help.

In the workroom, the rats missed the remains of old Bourjac's luncheons; the rats squeaked ravenously. . . . As she strove to scream, with the voice that was barely audible, she felt that she could resign herself to death were she but alone. She could not stir a limb or draw a breath apart from the man. She craved at last less ardently for life than for space —the relief of escaping, even for a single moment, from the oppression of contact. It became horrible, the contact, as revolting as if she had never loved him. The ceaseless contact maddened her. The quaking of his body, the clamminess of his flesh, the smell of his person poisoning the darkness, seemed to her the eternities of Hell.

Bourjac lay awaiting his wife's return for more than a fortnight. Then he sent for her mother, and learnt that the "aunt in Rouen" had been buried nearly three years.

The old man was silent.

"It is a coincidence," added the visitor hesitatingly, "that Monsieur Legrand has also disappeared. People are always ringing my bell to inquire where he is."

As soon as he was able to rise, Bourjac left for Paris; and, as the shortest route to the station was by the garden gate, he passed the workroom on his way. He nodded, thinking of the time that he had wasted there, but he did not go inside—he was too impatient to find Laure, and, incidentally, to shoot Legrand.

Though his quest failed, he never went back to the cottage; he could not have borne to live in it now. He tried to let it, but the little house was not everybody's money, and it stood empty for many years; indeed, before it was reoccupied Bourjac was dead and forgotten.

When the new owners planned their renovations, they had the curiosity to open a mildewed cabinet in an outhouse, and uttered a cry of dismay. Not until then was the "last effect" attained; but there were two skeletons, instead of one.

XIII

THE LADY OF LYONS'

THE jovial solicitor who smacked his clients on the back had absconded, and the minor poet had no longer fifty pounds per annum. Although he was a minor poet, which—strangely enough—is a term of contempt in this country, though we are enjoined to be grateful for even small mercies, he was as human as minor novelists and minor critics, and he suffered. Also he woke; he realised how small had been the world's demand for the wares in which he dealt—he acknowledged that for twenty years he had been living on his little income, not on his little books.

His name was Smith. It was, perhaps, one of the reasons why his poetry was unread. Only a reviewer possessed of unusual courage could have discovered "the great poetry of Mr. Smith." Only a poet devoid of commercial instincts could have failed to adopt a nom de guerre.

In the face of disaster Mr. Smith did not make precisely this reflection, but he reflected painfully that a lack of commercial ability was no longer a matter to be recognised with a smile. He stood among the daffodils in the village garden, and asked Heaven what would become of him. He was seven-and-thirty; the only craft that he had learnt was use-less; and he had to earn his bread-and-cheese.

As Heaven returned no answer, he sought the advice of friends. He was a lovable creature, though a writing man, and his friends were sympa-thetic. They all invited him to dinner, and assured him warmly that they would beaɪ his necessities in mind. If anything turned up, he might rely upon their telegraphing to him. Being of a trustful dis-position, Mr. Smith returned to the daffodils, encouraged.

And they withered while he waited for a telegram.

When they hung their heads, he sought advice again. This time his friends did not invite him to dinner, but they pointed out to him, lest he over-looked it, that he was a poet—in other words, that he was a difficult person to serve. "You have no experience, you see," they said frankly. "You are intelligent, but you have no experience, Robert." When a man is untravelled in the groove that we ourselves tread, we say that he has "no experience."

One afternoon the poet went abroad. The journey cost him a penny, and he travelled from Charing Cross as far as the Bank. He was bound for an office in Lombard Street, and as he called by appointment, a clerk showed him promptly to Mr. Hutton's private room.

The business man who received him had once been a little boy in a sailor suit, and he and Robert had played together in a nursery. To-day he had numerous financial irons in the fire, and one of them required an obedient gentleman to watch it. Affection suggested Robert for the post. The duties were simple, and the salary was slight, but if the iron came out in good condition, there was to be a slice of the iron, too.

They chatted for a long while. Robert was admitted to some confidences about the other irons—the patents, and the shares, and the concessions. All the time that he listened he was seeing the business man as a little boy in a sailor suit again, and was awestruck to hear the little boy talking so glibly of such mysteries. Blankly he felt that he himself had omitted to grow up; he decided that people were right in declaring that he had no experience; it appeared to him suddenly that he had learnt nothing in his life. But, of course, he had learnt many things, though never the most important one—how to make money.

Often they were interrupted by the telephone bell, and during one of the colloquies on the telephone Mr. Hutton seemed depressed. Robert feared he was being browbeaten until he hung up the receiver, and announced, smiling, that he had "made five

hundred pounds by that conversation." It was
miraculous. Robert had not made five hundred
pounds by twenty years of work.

"Let's go out and get a cup of coffee," said Mr.
Hutton, and piloted the poet through a maze of
alleys to a retiring doorway. "What will you have
to drink?" The poet discovered that after two
o'clock "a cup of coffee" in the City is generally a
synonym for a whisky-and-soda.

The little bar was crowded, and he was surprised
at seeing such a number of business men doing nothing so leisurely. One man to whom he was introduced asked him if he knew how the "House" closed,
but he did not even know what it meant. They discoursed in groups, and a strange language; Robert
was flooded by compassion for the barmaid. All
expounded different views, and all the views were
equally unintelligible to him. The only point of
unanimity he perceived was the wisdom of having "a
fiver each way." As often as anybody entered, the
several groups waved hands, and the newcomer
accepted a whisky-and-soda with a piece of lemon in
it, among the group he fancied best. On leaving,
Mr. Hutton remarked that he had "sometimes made
as much as a thousand pounds by dropping in there."
Robert reeled.

Soon he went every day to the strange land where
men talked a language that he did not know. It had
been decided that he should watch the iron in the

neighbourhood, so that Mr. Hutton might extend a guiding hand without discomfort, and an office was rented in Eastcheap. Eastcheap is a sour-smelling thoroughfare into which dirty loafers emerge from the courts of Billingsgate in order that they may have more room to spit. Distressing as Robert found it to sit in the office, he found it more distressing to go out.

Of course not many people see the City. Myriads saw it once, but that was when they came there in their youth. Few are to be discovered in the City who remember how it looks. Occasionally a clerk in his first berth may be found who sees the City, but he is not promised to the casual searcher, for City clerks as a body are observant in the streets of one thing only. They observe neckties. This passion, to which the hosiers of the district pander inordinately, was displayed to the poet between the hours of one and two, wet or fine. From desk to food, from food to desk, streamed the black multitude, expressionless, torpid and unseeing, until neckties flaunted in a window; then the vacant faces brightened, and there was a block. The rule of the pavement is known everywhere excepting in the City, where it is most needed; but at the hosiers' windows pedestrianism became more than an effort—it became a feat.

Robert's eyes had no custom in them; Robert did see the City, and he was unhappier than he had poetry to tell; for that matter, he did not try to tell it. He wrote nothing now but figures, and commercially ungrammatical epistles which took him a long time to compose. For twenty years he had believed his rushlight was a star—he had done with illusion at last. Illusion was in its grave, and the Failure laid his hope of laurels on the top. Yet he thought tenderly of Illusion. The funeral was over, but he mourned. He had embraced a new career, but he did not love it. Although he repeated that the past was dead, he could not prevent its ghost haunting Eastcheap. There were moments when it chilled the iron.

Often, as he forced his dreary way to luncheon, it walked beside him. He lunched sometimes with his preserver in the restaurants of the Employers. Generally he lunched with the ghost in the restaurants of the Employed. He noted that in the former the meat was tainted less frequently. On the other hand, the Employed were served by clean, quiet girls instead of by sleezy, vociferous waiters.

One afternoon he lunched at an establishment that he had not tried before. The ghost had been insistent all the morning. He found a vacant seat, hung up his hat, and examined the bill of fare. He was in one of the more modest restaurants of Messrs. Lyons, and around him young men and women with blank faces chumped beef-steak pudding, and read six-penny editions of the novels that are written for them. The girl beside him ordered apple-tart. Her voice was pleasant, and momentarily he regretted that in reading she leant her cheek upon her palm, for she hid her profile. It should have been a pretty profile, to match her voice. Moved by an impulse of curiosity, he glanced at the page she pondered, and then he dropped the menu: she was reading his own verse!

"Good God!" he exclaimed.

"I *beg* your pardon?" said the girl, surveying him with dignity.

"I apologise," stammered the poet; "I was startled."

Evidently she found his excuse inadequate, and he was thankful that at this moment they were left with the table to themselves. "I meant that I was startled to see the book you were reading," he explained.

"I see nothing startling in it," said the lady, still frigid.

He felt that she might have expressed herself more happily, but he was in no position to rebuke her. "Of course in one sense it isn't startling at all," he concurred; "in fact, it's very feeble."

"I am afraid I can't agree with you," rejoined his reader; and the haughtiness of her contradiction warmed his heart.

"You can't mean you really like it?"

"I like it very much." She had grey eyes that

challenged him scornfully; he sunned himself in her disdain.

"Did you buy it?" he asked, a tremor in his tone.

"Really—!" she began. But his air was so respectful that she added the next instant, "Yes, for twopence, second-hand."

"Ah!" said the poet. "Still it's a most extraordinary occurrence."

She looked away from him with a frown; her attention was divided between his verse and the apple-tart. Robert sat a prey to temptation. To melt her by avowing himself would be ridiculous, but agreeable. Succumbing, he murmured:

"To tell you the truth, I am glad you like the book."

"Eh?" she said. "Why?"

"Because I wrote it."

It should have been a dramatic moment, but the girl bungled her part and disbelieved him.

Fully five minutes were devoted to convincing her. However, the five minutes brought such a flutter of pink to her cheeks, so tender a glow into her eyes, that the time was by no means wasted.

"I couldn't expect to meet a poet in the City," she pleaded.

"And certainly I couldn't expect to meet my Gentle Reader here," said Robert. He examined the slim volume ruefully.

"In such good condition, and only twopence!" he complained.

"If it had been more I mightn't have bought it," she said.

He found himself resigned that the book had been marked down to twopence.

She told him that she wrote shorthand in an office in Cornhill. Eastcheap lay in the same direction, and after she had gone he felt it would have been pleasurable to walk some of the way beside her.

He was sorry, too, that he had omitted to inquire if she irradiated the restaurant daily.

On the morrow he betook himself to Lyons' with hope. He descried the lady at a distant table, and it had the charm of vacant chairs. There was no reason why he should ignore them.

"You are often in the City, then?" she asked as he sat down.

"I come every day," said Robert, and seeing she was mystified, he added, "I am in an office here, like you."

But plainly this mystified her more still. "Do you mean you are in business?"

"Truly," he told her. "I think I shall have roast beef."

"I should try the mutton," she said. "But you are a poet?"

"I used to fancy myself one."

It was very absurd, but before they paid their bills

he was informing her that he had divorced his Muse, and was in a foreign land alone. This time they left the restaurant together.

"That, O foreigner," said the lady of Lyons', "is the Royal Exchange!"

"I know," said Robert. "But what do they exchange in it?"

"I have no idea," she confessed. "If you like, we will ask a policeman."

"A curious thing about policemen," remarked the poet, "is that if you want a civil answer, you must avoid putting your question civilly. They are, conspicuously, a class who respect rudeness. How long have you been coming to the City, to learn so much about it?"

"I have been coming to the City for nine years," she said, "and I have learnt a great deal. I know now where the Tower is, and which of the benches under the trees makes you feel most Harrison Ainsworthy. And I know the shop in Cornhill that sells the best twopenny tarts. They are small, but peerless."

"If you hadn't bought my verses you might have had another," sighed Robert. "Some day, when I have made my fortune, I shall give you one."

"Thank you," she said. "I suppose you know what you are looking at across the road?"

"I am looking at a book shop," replied the poet.

"You were meant to see the Mansion House,"

demurred his guide, "where the Lord Mayor lives."

"I do not like Lord Mayors," said Robert, "they never ask me to their literary dinners."

"They are punished for it," said the girl. "Once a year at midnight they drop their little glass slippers, and their beautiful coach turns back into a pumpkin."

"It serves them right," said the poet vengefully.

But they were not always so foolish at this. To meet at luncheon became their custom, and sometimes their confidences were quite practical. By dint of lunching hurriedly on occasion, they made time to reach the Tower together, and he approved her taste in benches. It was on the bench one day when the sun shone that she told him her history. Her history was so commonplace that she apologised for relating it, and her surprise was vast that he fell to reverie.

"Why," he cried, "we have found a Moral! It is you who are to be pitied, not I. What have I to mourn in the City? I have buried nothing here but the gift of making little verses. But you, you have buried the divinest gift of the gods, your beautiful youth! You have never had any pleasure in your life, yet you are content. I am ashamed."

Not long afterwards his preserver exclaimed:

"Bobbie, I think you're getting acclimatised. You're putting your back into it—if you don't take care you'll make money!"

"I aim at making money," said the poet with commercial staidness; and added irresponsibly, "I want to buy twopenny tarts."

It was just like him, to bid farewell to verse-making, and then to find his best poetry in the City. There are dreamers who would turn every opportunity to disadvantage.

But the iron is shaping so well that when it becomes a limited liability company with another manager, Robert's slice should be substantial.

We may imagine him going back to the daffodils.

It is not impossible that there will be orange blossoms.

And in the meantime there is certainly the luncheon hour.

XIV

HOW TRICOTRIN SAW LONDON

THERE was a day when Tricotrin had eighty francs, and he said to Pitou, who was equally prosperous, "Good-bye to follies, for we have arrived at an epoch in our careers! Do not let us waste our substance on trivial pleasures, or paying the landlord—let us make it a provision for our future!"

"I rejoice to hear you speak for once like a practical man," returned Pitou. "Do you recommend landed property, or an old-age pension?"

"I would suggest, rather, that we apply our riches to some educational purpose, such as travel," explained the poet, producing a railway company's handbill. "By this means we shall enlarge our minds, and somebody has pretended that 'knowledge is power'—it must have been the proprietor of a school. Mon vieux, it is not for nothing that we have 'l'entente cordiale'—one may now spend a Sunday in London at the price of one of Ivonne's hats."

"They say that these London Sunday trips are a plot of the English Government to exterminate us,"

218

demurred Pitou, "since it is well known that none but English people could survive a Sunday in London."

"What a base suspicion!" cried Tricotrin. "Are we not offered the choice of Eastbourne—that rollicking resort of the fine flower of English fashion?"

"Well, your synopsis will be considered, and reported on in due course," announced the composer, after a slight pause; "but at the moment of going to press we would rather buy another hat for Ivonne."

And as Ivonne also thought that this would be better for him, it was decided that Tricotrin should set forth alone.

His departure for a foreign country was a solemn event. A small party of the Montmartrois had marched with him to the station, and more than once, in view of their anxious faces, the young man acknowledged mentally that he was committed to a harebrained scheme.

"Heaven protect thee, my comrade!" faltered Pitou. "Is thy vocabulary safely in thy pocket? Remember that 'un bock' is 'glassofbeer.'"

"Here is a small packet of chocolate," murmured Lajeunie, embracing him, "chocolate is very sustaining; in England, I am assured, nothing to eat can be obtained on Sunday."

"And listen!" shouted Goujaud; "on no account take off thy hat to strangers, nor laugh in the streets;

the first is 'mad' over there, and the second is 'immoral.' May le bon Dieu have thee in his keeping! We count the hours till thy return!"

Then the train sped out into the night, and the poet realized that home and friends were left behind.

He would have been less than a poet if, in the first few minutes, the pathos of the situation had not gripped him by the throat. Vague, elusive fancies stirred his brain; he remembered the franc that he owed at the Faisan d'Or, and wondered if Madame would speak gently of him were he lost at sea. Tender memories of past loves dimmed his eyes, and he reflected how poignant it would be to perish before the papers would give him any obituary notices. Regarding his fellow passengers, he lamented that none of them was a beautiful girl, for it was an occasion on which woman's sympathy would have been sweet, indeed he proceeded to invent some of the things that they might have said to each other. Inwardly he was still resenting the faces of his travelling companions when the train reached Dieppe.

"It is material for my biography," he soliloquised, as he crept down the gangway: " 'Few who saw the young man step firmly on to the good ship's deck conjectured the emotions that tore his heart; few recognised him to be Tricotrin, whose work was in 1907 practically unknown!' " But as a matter of fact he did arouse conjectures of a kind, for when the boat moved from the quay, he could not resist the opportunity to murmur, "My France, farewell!" with an appropriate gesture.

His repose during the night was fitful, and when Victoria was reached at last, he was conscious of some bodily fatigue.   However, his mind was never slow to receive impressions, and he whipped out his note-book on the platform. He wrote, "The English People are very prompt of action. One day it was discerned that le Gare Victoria was capable of improvement; no sooner was the fact detected than an army of contractors was feverishly enlarging it." Pleased that his journey was already yielding such good results, the poet lit a caporal, and sauntered through the yard.

Though the sky promised a fine Sunday, his view of London at this early hour was not inspiriting. He loitered blankly, debating which way to wander. Presently the outlook brightened—he observed a very dainty pair of shoes and ankles coming through the station doors.   Fearing that the face might be unworthy of them, he did not venture to raise his gaze until the girl had nearly reached the gate, but when he took the risk, he was rewarded by the discovery that her features were as piquante as her feet.

She came towards him slowly, and now he remarked that she had a grudge against Fate; her pretty lips were compressed, her beautiful eyes gloomy with grievance, the fairness of her brow was darkened by a frown. "Well," mused Tricotrin, "though the object of my visit is educational, the exigencies of my situation clearly compel me to ask this young lady to direct me somewhere. Can I summon up enough English before she has passed?"

It was a trying moment, for already she was nearly abreast of him. Forgetful of Goujaud's instructions, as well as of most of the phrases that had been committed to memory, the poet swept off his hat, and stammered, "Mees, I beg your pardon!"

She turned the aggrieved eyes to him inquiringly. Although she had paused, she made no answer. Was his accent so atrocious as all that? For a second they regarded each other dumbly, while a blush of embarrassment mantled the young man's cheeks. Then, with a little gesture of apology, the girl said in French—

"I do not speak English, monsieur."

"Oh, le bon Dieu be praised!" said Tricotrin, for all the world as if he had been back on the Boulevard Rochechouart. "I was dazed with travel, or I should have recognised you were a Frenchwoman. Did you, too, leave Paris last night, mademoiselle?"

"Oh, no," said the girl pensively, "I have been in London for months. I hoped to meet a friend who wrote that she would arrive this morning, but"—she sighed—"she has not come!"

"Doubtless she will arrive to-night instead; I should have no anxiety. You may be certain she will arrive to-night, and this contretemps will be forgotten."

She pouted. "I was looking forward so much to seeing her! To a stranger who cannot speak the language, London is as triste as a tomb. To-day, I was to have had a companion, and now——"

"Indeed, I sympathise with you," replied Tricotrin. "But is it really so—London is what you describe? You alarm me! I am here absolutely alone. Where, then, shall I go this morning?"

"There are churches," she said, after some reflection.

"And besides?"

"W-e-ll, there are other churches."

"Of course, such things can be seen in Paris also," demurred Tricotrin. "It is not essential to travel to a foreign land to say one's prayers. If I may take the liberty of applying to you, in which direction would you recommend me to turn my steps? For example, where is Soho—is it too far for a walk?"

"No, monsieur, it is not very far—it is the quarter in which I lodge."

"And do you return there now?" he asked eagerly.

"What else is there for me to do? My friend has not come, and——"

"Mademoiselle," exclaimed the poet. "I entreat you to have mercy on a compatriot! Permit me, at least, to seek Soho in your company—do not, I implore you, leave me homeless and helpless in a strange country! I notice an eccentric vehicle which instinct whispers is an English 'hansom.' For years I have aspired to drive in an English hansom once! It is in your power to fulfil my dream with effulgence. Will you consent to instruct the acrobat who is performing with a whip, and to take a seat in the English hansom beside me?"

"Monsieur," responded the pretty girl graciously, "I shall be charmed;" and romantic as the incident appears, the next minute they were driving along Victoria Street together.

"The good kind fairies have certainly taken me under their wings," declared Tricotrin, as he admired his companion's profile. "It was worth enduring the pangs of exile, to meet with such kindness as you have shown me!"

"I am afraid you will speedily pronounce the fairies fickle," she said, "for our drive will soon be over, and you will find Soho no fairyland."

"How comes it that your place of residence is so unsuitable to you, mademoiselle?"

"I lodge in the neighbourhood of the coiffeur's where I am engaged, monsieur—where I handle the 'tails' and 'transformations.' Our specialty is artificial eyelashes; the attachment is quite invisible—and the result, absolutely ravishing! No," she added hurriedly, "I am not wearing a pair myself; these are quite natural, word of honour! But we undertake to impart to any eyes the gaze soulful, or the twinkle coquettish, as the customer desires—as an artist, I assure you that these expressions are due, less to the eyes themselves than to the shade, and especially the form, of the lashes. Many a woman has entered our saloon entirely insignificant, and turned the heads of all the men in the street a quarter of an hour later, when she left."

"You interest me, profoundly," said Tricotrin. "At the same time, I shall never know in future whether I am being thrilled by a woman's eyes or by the handiwork of her coiffeur. I say 'in future,' for here and now, believe me, I entertain no doubt as to the source of my sensations."

She rewarded him for this by a glance that dizzied him, and soon afterwards the hansom came to a standstill amid an overpowering odour of cheese.

"We have arrived!" she proclaimed; "so it is now that we part, monsieur. For me there is the little lodging—for you the enormous London. It is Soho —wander where you will! There are restaurants hereabout where one may breakfast at a modest price. Accept my thanks for your escort, and let us say 'adieu.' "

"Are the restaurants so unsavoury that you decline to honour them?" he questioned.

"Comment?"

"Will you not bear me company? Or, better still, will you not let me command a breakfast for two to be sent to your apartment, and invite me to rest after my journey?"

She hesitated. "My apartment is very humble," she said, "and—well, I have never done a thing like that! It would not be correct. What would you think of me if I consented?"

"I will think all that you would have me think," vowed Tricotrin. "Come, take pity on me! Ask me in, and afterwards we will admire the sights of London together. Where shall I go to order the breakfast?"

"As for that," she said, "there is no necessity—I have a breakfast for two already prepared. Enfin, it is understood—we are to be good comrades, and nothing more? Will you give yourself the trouble of entering, monsieur?"

The bedroom to which they mounted was shabby, but far from unattractive. The mantelshelf was brightened with flowers, a piano was squeezed into a corner, and Tricotrin had scarcely put aside his hat when he was greeted by the odour of most excellent coffee.

"If this is London," he cried, "I have no fault to find with the city! I own it is abominably selfish of me, but I cannot bring myself to regret that your friend failed to arrive this morning; indeed, I shudder to think what would have become of me if we had not met! Will you mention the name that is to figure in my benizons?"

"My name is 'Rosalie Durand,' monsieur."

"And mine is 'Gustave Tricotrin,' mademoiselle—always your servant! In Paris, at this moment, there are men who picture me, I do not doubt, tramping the pavement, desolate. Not one of them but would envy me from his heart if he could see my situation!"

"It might have fallen out worse, I admit," said the girl. "My own day was at the point of being dull to tears—and here I am chattering as if I hadn't a grief in the world! Let me persuade you to take another croissant!"

"Fervently I wish that appearances were not deceptive!" said Tricotrin, who required little persuasion. "Is it indiscreet to inquire to what griefs you allude? Upon my word, your position appears a very pretty one! Where do those dainty shoes pinch you?"

"They are not easy on foreign soil, monsieur. When I reflect that you go back to-night, that to-morrow you will be again in Paris, I could gnash my teeth with jealousy."

"But, ma foi," returned Tricotrin, "to a girl of brains, like yourself, Paris is always open. Are there no customers for eyelashes in France? Why condemn yourself to gnash with jealousy when there is a living to be earned at home?"

"There are several reasons," she said; "for one thing, I am an extravagant little hussy, and I haven't saved enough money for my ticket."

"I have heard no reason yet! At the moment my pocket is nicely lined—you might return with me this evening."

"Are you mad by any chance?" she laughed.

"It seems to me the natural course. What hint of insanity is there about it?"

"Well, I should not be free to go like that, even if I took your money. I am a business woman, you see, who does not sacrifice her intersts to her sentiment. What is your own career, Monsieur Tricotrin?"

"I am a poet. And when I am back in Paris I shall write verse about you. The title shall be 'One Day in London'; I shall describe Peeccadeelly and the Lor' Maire as they present themselves to him who views them dazzled by the girl he loves."

"Forbidden ground!" she cried, admonishing him with a finger. "No dazzle!"

"I apologise," said Tricotrin; "you shall find me a poet of my word. Why, I declare," he exclaimed, glancing from the window, "it has begun to rain!"

"Well, fortunately, we have plenty of time; there is all day for our excursion, and we can wait for the weather to improve. If you do not object to smoking a cigarette while I sing, monsieur, I propose a little music to go on with."

And it turned out that this singular assistant of a hairdresser had a very sympathetic voice, and no contemptible répertoire. Although the sky had now broken its promise shamefully and the downpour continued, Tricotrin found nothing to complain of. By mid-day one would have said that they had been comrades for years. By luncheon both had even ceased to regard the rain. And before evening approached, they had confided to each other their histories from the day of their birth.

Ascertaining that the basement boasted a smudgy servant girl, who was to be despatched for entrées and sauterne, Tricotrin drew up the menu of a magnificent dinner as the climax. It was conceded that at this repast he should be the host; and having placed him on oath behind a screen, Rosalie proceeded to make an elaborate toilette in honour of his entertainment.

Determined, as he had said, to prove himself a poet of his word, the young man remained behind the screen as motionless as a waxwork, but the temptation to peep was tremendous, and at the whispering of a silk petticoat he was unable to repress a groan.

"What ails you?" she demanded, the whispering suspended.

"I merely expire with impatience to meet you again."

"Monsieur, I am hastening to the trysting-place. And my costume will be suitable to the occasion, believe me!"

"In that case, if you are not quick, you will have

to wear crêpe. However, proceed! I can suffer
with the best of them . . . Are you certain that
I can be of no assistance? I feel selfish, idling here
like this. Besides, since I am able to see——"

"See?" she screamed.

"——see no reason why you should refuse my aid,
my plight is worse still! What are you doing now?"

"My hair," she announced.

"Surely it would not be improper for me to view a
head of hair?"

"Perhaps not, monsieur; but my head is on my
shoulders—which makes a difference!"

"Mademoiselle," sighed Tricotrin, "never have I
known a young lady whose head was on her
shoulders more tightly! May I crave one indulgence? My imprisonment would be less painful for
a cigarette, and I cannot reach the matches—will you
consent to pass them round the screen?"

"That is against the rules. But I will consent to
throw them over the top. Catch! Why don't you
say 'thank you'?"

"Because your unjust suspicion killed me. I now
need nothing but immortelles; and at dinner I will
compose my epitaph. If I am not mistaken, I already
smell the soup on the stairs."

And the soup had scarcely entered when his guest
presented herself. Paquin and the Fairy Godmother
would have approved her gown; as to her coiffeur, if
her employer could have seen it, he would have

wanted to put her in his window. Tricotrin gave her
his arm in stupefaction. "Upon my word," he
faltered, "you awe me! I am now overwhelmed
with embarrassment that I had the temerity to tease
you while you dressed. And what shall I say of the
host who is churl enough to welcome you in such a
shabby coat!"

The cork went pop, their tongues went nineteen to
the dozen, and the time went so rapidly that a little
clock on the chest of drawers became a positive
killjoy.

"By all the laws of dramatic effect," remarked the
poet, as they trifled with the almonds and raisins,
"you will now divulge that the fashionable lady before me is no 'Rosalie Durand,' of a hairdresser's
shop, but Mme. la Comtesse de Thrilling Mystery.
Every novel reader would be aware that at this stage
you will demand some dangerous service of me, and
that I shall forthwith risk my life and win your love."

"That is how it ought to be," she agreed, "without
doubt."

"Is it impossible?"

"That I can be a Countess?"

"Well, we will waive the 'Countess'; and for that
matter I will not insist on risking my life; but what
about the love?"

"Without the rest," she demurred, "the situation
would be too commonplace. When I can tell you
that I am a Countess I will say also that I love you;

to-night I am Rosalie Durand—your friend. By the way, now I come to think of it, I shall be all that you have seen in London!"

"Why, I declare, so you will!" exclaimed Tricotrin. "Really this is a nice thing! I come to England for the benefit of my education—and when it is almost time for me to return, I find that I have spent the whole of the day in a room."

"But you have at least had a unique experience?" she queried with a whimsical smile.

"Well, yes; my journey has certainly yielded an adventure that none of my acquaintances would credit!" he acknowledged. "Do you laugh at me?"

"Far from it; by and by I may even spare a tear for you—if you do not spoil the day by being clumsy at the end."

"Ah, Rosalie," cried the susceptible poet, "how can I bear the parting? What is France without you? I am no longer a Frenchman—my true home is now England! My heart will hunger for it, my thoughts will stretch themselves to it across the sea; banished to Montmartre, I shall mourn daily for the white cliffs of Albion, for Soho, and for you!"

"I, too, shall remember," she murmured. "But perhaps one of these days you will come to England again?"

"If a ticket could be paid for with devotion, I would come every Sunday; but how can I hope to amass enough money? Such things do not happen twice. No, I will not deceive myself—this is our farewell. See!" He rose, and turned the little clock with its face to the wall. "When that clock strikes, I must go to catch my train—in the meanwhile we will ignore the march of time. Farewells, tears, regrets, let us forget that they exist—let us drink the last glass together gaily, mignonne!"

They pledged each other with brave smiles, hand in hand. And now their chatter became fast and furious, to drown the clock's impatient tick.

The clockwork wheezed and whirred.

" 'Tis going to part us," shouted Tricotrin; "laugh, laugh, Beloved, so that we may not hear!"

"Kiss me," she cried; "while the hour strikes, you shall hold me in your arms!"

"Heaven," gasped the young man, as the brief embrace concluded, "how I wish it had been midnight!"

The next moment came the separation. He descended the stairs; at the window she waved her hand to him. And in the darkness of an "English hansom" the poet covered his face and wept.

"From our hearts we rejoice to have thee safely back!" they chorused in Montmartre. "And what did'st thou see in London?"

"Oh, mon Dieu, what noble sights!" exclaimed Tricotrin. "The Lor' Maire blazes with jewels like the Shah of Persia; and compared with Peeccadeelly, the Grands Boulevards are no wider than a hatband. Never in my life have I admired a city so much. Vive l'Entente Cordiale! Positively my brain whirls with all the splendours of London I have seen!"

XV

A MIRACLE IN MONTMARTRE

LAJEUNIE, the luckless novelist, went to Pitou, the unrecognised composer, saying, "I have a superb scenario for a revue. Let us join forces! I promise you we shall make a fortune; we shall exchange our attics for first floors of fashion, and be wealthy enough to wear sable overcoats and Panama hats at the same time." In ordinary circumstances, of course, Pitou would have collaborated only with Tricotrin, but Tricotrin was just then engrossed by a tragedy in blank verse and seven acts, and he said to them, "Make a fortune together by all means, my comrades; I should be unreasonable if I raised objections to having rich friends."

Accordingly the pair worked like heroes of biography, and, after vicissitudes innumerable, "Patatras" was practically accepted at La Coupole. The manager even hinted that Diane D'Esterre might be seen in the leading part. La Coupole, and D'Esterre! Pitou and Lajeunie could scarcely credit their ears. To be sure, she was no actress, and her voice was rather unpleasant, and she would probably want everything rewritten fifteen times before it satisfied her; but she was a beautiful woman, and all Paris paid to look at her when she graced a stage; and she had just ruined Prince Czernowitz, which gave her name an additional value. "Upon my word," gasped Pitou, "our luck seems as incredible, my dear Lajeunie, as the plot of any of your own novels! Come and have a drink!"

"I feel like Rodolphe at the end of 'La Vie de Bohème,'" he confided to Tricotrin in their garret one winter's night, as they went supperless to their beds. "Now that the days of privation are past, I recall them with something like regret. The shock of the laundress's totals, the meagre dinners at the Faisan d'Or, these things have a fascination now that I part from them. I do not wish to sound ungrateful, but I cannot help wondering if my millions will impair the taste of life to me."

"To me they will make it taste much better," said Tricotrin, "for I shall have somebody to borrow money from, and I shall get enough blankets. *Aïe,* how cold I am! Besides, you need not lose touch with Montmartre because you are celebrated—you can invite us all to your magnificent abode. Also, you can dine at the Faisan still, if sentiment pulls you that way."

"I shall certainly dine there," averred Pitou. "And I shall buy a house for my parents, with a peacock and some deer on the lawn. At the same time, a triumph is not without its pathos. I see my return to the Faisan—the old affections in my heart, the old greetings on my presence. I see Madame apologising for the cuisine, instead of reminding me that my credit is exhausted, and the waiter polishing my glass, instead of indicating the cheapest item on the menu. Such changes hurt!" He was much moved. "A fortune is not everything," he sighed, forgetting that his pockets were as empty as his stomach. "Poverty yielded joys which I no longer know."

The poet embraced him with emotion. "I rejoice to find that Fame has not spoilt your nature," he cried; and he, too, forgot the empty pockets, and that the contract from La Coupole had yet to come. "Yes, we had hard times together, you and I, and *I* am still a 'nobody'; but we shall be chums as long as we live. I feel that you can unbosom yourself to me, the poor bohemian, more freely than to any Immortal with whom you hobnob in scenes of splendour."

"Oh, indeed, indeed!" assented Pitou, weeping copiously, and getting between his ragged sheets. "You are as dear to me now as in the days of our struggles; I should curse my affluence if it made you doubt that! Good night, my brother; God bless you."

Half an hour crept by.

"Gustave!"

"Eh bien?" said Tricotrin, looking towards the other bed. "Not asleep yet?"

"I cannot sleep—hunger is gnawing at me."

"Ah, what a relentless realist is this hunger," complained the poet, "how it destroys one's illusions!"

"Is there nothing to eat in the attic?"

"Not a crumb—I am ravenous myself. But I recall a broken cigarette in my waistcoat pocket; let us cut it in halves!"

They strove, shivering, to appease their pangs by slow whiffs of a caporal, and while they supped in this unsatisfactory fashion, there came an impetuous knocking at the street door.

"It must be that La Coupole has sent you a sack of gold to go on with," Tricotrin opined. "Put your head out and see."

"It is Lajeunie," announced the composer, withdrawing from the window with chattering teeth. "What the devil can he want? I suppose I must go down and let him in."

"Perhaps we can get some more cigarettes from him," said Tricotrin; "it might have been worse."

But when the novelist appeared, the first thing he stammered was, "Give me a cigarette, one of you fellows, or I shall die!"

"Well, then, dictate your last wishes to us!" returned Pitou. "Do you come here under the impression that the house is a tobacconist's? What is the matter with you, what is up?"

"For three hours," snuffled Lajeunie, who looked half frozen and kept shuddering violently, "for three hours I have been pacing the streets questioning whether I should break the news to you to-night or not. In one moment I told myself that it would be better to withhold it till the morning; in the next I felt that you had a right to hear it without delay. Hour after hour, in the snow, I turned the matter over in my mind, and——"

"Mon Dieu," exclaimed Pitou, "is this a feuilleton at so much a column? Come to the point!"

Lajeunie beat his breast. "I am distracted," he faltered, "I am no longer master of myself. Listen! It occurred to me this evening that I might do worse than pay a visit to La Coupole and inquire if a date was fixed yet for the production. Well, I went. For a long time I could obtain no interview, I could obtain no appointment—the messenger came back with evasive answers. I am naturally quick at smelling a rat—I have the detective's instinct—and I felt that there was something wrong. My heart began to fail me."

"For mercy's sake," groaned his unhappy collaborator, "explode the bomb and bury my fragments! Enough of these literary introductions! Did you see the manager, or didn't you?"

"I did see the miscreant, the bandit-king, I saw

him in the street! For I was not to be put off—I
waited till he came out. Well, my friend, to com-
press the tragedy into one act, our hope is shattered
—'Patatras' is again refused!"

"Oh, heavens!" moaned Pitou, and fell back upon
the mattress as white as death.

"What explanation did he make?" cried Tricotrin;
"what is the reason?"

"The reason is that D'Esterre is an imbecile—she
finds the part unworthy of her talents. A part on
which I have lavished all the wealth of my invention
—she finds it beneath her; she said she would 'break
her contract rather than play it'! Well, D'Esterre
is the trump-card of his season—he would throw
over the whole of the Academy sooner than lose
D'Esterre. Since she objects to figuring in 'Patatras,'
'Patatras' is waste-paper to him. Alas! who would
be an author! I would rather shovel coke, or cut
corns for a living! He himself admitted that there
was no fault to find with the revue, but, 'You know
well, monsieur, that we must humour D'Esterre'! I
asked him if he would try to bring her to her senses,
but it seems that there have been a dozen discussions
already—he is sick of the subject. Now it is settled
—our manuscript will be banged back at us, and we
may rip!"

"O, my mother!" moaned Pitou, "O, the peacock
and the deer!"

"What's that you say?" asked Lajeunie. "Are

you positive that you haven't got a cigarette anywhere?"

"I am positive that I have nothing," proclaimed Pitou vehemently, "nothing in life but a broken heart! Oh, you did quite right to come to me, but now leave me—leave me to perish. I have no words, I am stricken. The next time you see me it will be in the Morgue. Mon Dieu, that beautiful wretch, that creature without conscience, or a note in her voice—by a shrug of her elegant shoulders she condemns me to the Seine!"

"Ah, do not give way!" exclaimed Tricotrin, leaping out of bed. "Courage, my poor fellow, courage! Are there not other managers in Paris?"

"There are—and 'Patatras' has been refused by them. La Coupole was our last chance, and it has collapsed. We have no more to expect—it is all over! Is it not so, Lajeunie?"

"All over!" sobbed Lajeunie, bowing his head on the washhand-stand. " 'Patatras' is dead!"

Then for some seconds the only sound to be heard in the attic was the laboured breathing of the three young men's despair.

At last Tricotrin, drawing himself upright in his tattered nightshirt, said, with a gesture of dignity, "Well, the case may justify me—in the present situation it appears to me that I have the right to use my influence with D'Esterre!"

A signal from Mars could scarcely have caused a

more profound sensation. Pitou and Lajeunie regarded him with open mouths. "Your influence?" echoed Pitou; "your influence? I was not aware that you had ever met her."

"No," rejoined the poet darkly; "I have not met her. But there are circumstances in my life which entitle me to demand a service of this triumphant woman. Do not question me, my friends—what I shall say to her must remain a secret even from you; I declare, however, that nobody has a stronger claim on her than Gustave Tricotrin, the poor penny-a-liner whom she does not know!"

The sudden intervention—to say nothing of its literary flavour—so excited the collaborators that they nearly wrung his hands off; and Lajeunie, who recognised a promising beginning for another serial, was athirst for further hints.

"She has perhaps committed a murder, that fair fiend?" he inquired rapturously.

"Perhaps," replied Tricotrin.

"In that case she dare refuse you nothing."

"Why not, since I have never heard of it?"

"I was only jesting," said the novelist. "In sober earnest, I conjecture that you are married to her, like Athos to Miladi. As you stand there, with that grave air, you strongly resemble Athos."

"Nevertheless, Athos did not marry a woman to whom he had not spoken, and I repeat that I have never spoken to D'Esterre in my life."

"Well," said Lajeunie, "I have too much respect for your wishes to show any curiosity. Besides, by an expert the mystery is to be divined—before the story opens, you rendered her some silent aid, and your name will remind her of a great heroism?"

"I have never rendered her any aid at all," demurred Tricotrin, "and there is not the slightest reason to suppose that she has ever heard my name. But again, I have an incontestable right to demand a service of her, and for the sake of the affection I bear you both, I shall go to do it."

"When Tricotrin thinks that he is living in 'The Three Musketeers' it is useless to try to pump him," said Pitou; "let us content ourselves with what we are told! Is it not enough? Our fate is in D'Esterre's hands, and he is in a position to ask a favour of her. What more can we want?"

But he could not resist putting a question on his own account after Lajeunie had skipped downstairs.

"Gustave, why did you never mention to me that you knew D'Esterre?"

"Morbleu! how often must I say that I do *not* know her?"

"Well—how shall I express it?—that some episode in your career gave you a claim on her consideration?"

"Because, by doing so, I should have both violated a confidence, and re-opened a wound which still burns," said Tricotrin, more like Athos than ever.

"Only the urgency of your need, my comrade, could induce me to take the course that I project! Now let me sleep, for to-morrow I must have all my wits."

It was, however, five o'clock already, and before either of them had slept long the steps of the Passage des Abbesses clattered with feet on their way to the laundries, and vendors of delicacies were bawling suggestions for appetising breakfasts.

"Not only do the shouts of these monsters disturb my slumber, but they taunt my starvation!" yawned the poet. "Yet, now I come to think of it, I have an appointment with a man who has sworn to lend me a franc, so perhaps I had better get up before he is likely to have spent it. I shall call upon D'Esterre in the afternoon, when she returns from her drive. What is your own programme?"

"My first attempt will be at a laiterie in the Rue St. Rustique, where I am inclined to think I may get credit for milk and a roll if I swagger."

"Capital," said Tricotrin; "things are looking up with us both! And if I raise the franc, there will be half of it for you to squander on a recherché luncheon. Meet me in the Place Dancourt in an hour's time. So long!"

Never had Mlle. D'Esterre looked more captivating than when her carriage brought her back that day. She wore—but why particularise? Suffice it, that she had just been photographed. As she stepped to the pavement she was surprised by the obeisance of a shabby young man, who said in courtly tones, "Mademoiselle, may I beg the honour of an interview with you? I come from La Coupole." Having bestowed a glance of annoyance on him, she invited him to ascend the stairs, and a minute later Tricotrin was privileged to watch her take off her hat before the mirror.

"Eh bien?" she inquired, "what's the trouble there now; what do they want?"

"So far as I know, mademoiselle," returned the intruder deferentially, "they want nothing but your beauty and your genius; but I myself want infinitely more—I want your attention and your pity. Let me explain without delay that I do not represent the Management, and that when I said I came from La Coupole I should have added that I did not come from the interior."

"Upon my word!" she said sharply; "Who are you, then?"

"I am Tricotrin, mademoiselle—Gustave Tricotrin, at your feet. I have two comrades, the parents of 'Patatras'; you have refused to play in it, and I fear they will destroy themselves. I come to beg you to save their lives."

"Monsieur," exclaimed the lady, and her eyes were brilliant with temper, "all that I have to say about 'Patatras' I have said. The part gave me the hump!"

"And yet," continued the suppliant firmly, "I hope

to induce you to accept it. I am an author myself, and I assure you that it teems with opportunities which you may have overlooked in a casual reading."

"It is stupid!"

"As you would play it, I predict that it would be a triumph."

"And the music is no good!"

"If I may venture to differ from you, the music is melodious in the extreme—Pitou is my lifelong friend."

"I appreciate the argument," she said, with fine irony. "But you can scarcely expect me to play a part I don't like in order to please you."

"Frankly, that is just what I dare to expect," replied the poet. "I think that you may consent for my sake."

"Oh, really? For *your* sake? Would you mind mentioning why, before you go?"

"Because, mademoiselle," said Tricotrin, folding his arms, "in years gone by, you ruined me!"

"Mon Dieu!" she gasped, and she did not doubt that she was in the presence of a lunatic.

"Do not rush to the bell!" he begged; "if it will allay your panic, I will open the door and address you from the landing! I am not insane, and I solemnly assert that I am one of the men who have had the honour of being ruined by you."

"I have never seen you in my life before!"

"I know it, I even admit that I attach no blame to

you in the matter. Nevertheless, you cost me two thousand, five hundred, and forty-three francs, and—as you may judge by my costume—I do not own the Crédit Lyonnais. If you will deign to hear my story, I guarantee that it will convince you. Do you permit me to proceed?"

The beauty nodded wonderingly, and the shabby young man continued in the following words:

"As I have said, I am an author; I shall 'live' by my poetry, but I exist by my prose—in fact, I turn my pen to whatever promises a dinner, be it a sonnet to the Spring, or a testimonial to a hair restorer. One summer, when dinners had been even more elusive than usual, I conceived the idea of calling attention to my talents by means of an advertisement. In reply, I received a note bidding me be on the third step of the Madeleine at four o'clock the following day, and my correspondent proved to be a gentleman whose elegant apparel proclaimed him a Parisian of the Boulevards.

" 'You are Monsieur Gustave Tricotrin?' he inquired.

" 'I have that misfortune, monsieur,' said I. We adjourned to a café, and after a preliminary chat, from which he deduced that I was a person of discretion, he made me a proposal.

"He said, 'Monsieur Tricotrin, it is evident that you and I were designed to improve each other's condition; *your* dilemma is that, being unknown, you cannot dispose of your stories—*mine* is that, being known so well, I am asked for more stories than I have time to write. I suggest that you shall write some for me. *I* will sign them, they will be paid for in accordance with my usual terms, and you shall receive a generous share of the money. I need not impress upon you that I am speaking in the strictest confidence, and that you must never breathe a word about our partnership, even to the wife of your bosom.'

" 'Monsieur,' I returned, 'I have no wife to breathe to, and my bosom is unsurpassed as a receptacle for secrets.'

" 'Good,' he said. 'Well, without beating about the bush, I will tell you who I am.' He then uttered a name that made me jump, and before we parted it was arranged that I should supply him with a tale immediately as a specimen of my abilities.

"This tale, which I accomplished the same evening, pleased him so well that he forthwith gave me an order for two more. I can create a plot almost as rapidly as a debt, and before long I had delivered manuscripts to him in such wholesale quantities that if I had been paid cash for them, I should have been in a position to fête Montmartre. It was his custom, however, to make excuses and payments on account, and as we were capital friends by now, I never demurred.

"Well, things went on in this fashion until one day

he hinted to me that I had provided him with enough manuscripts to last him for two years; his study was lumbered with evidence of my talent, and his market, after all, was not unlimited. He owed me then close upon three thousand francs, and it was agreed that he should discharge the liability by weekly install-ments. Enfin, I was content enough—I foresaw an ample income for two years to come, and renewed leisure to win immortality by my epics. I trust that my narrative does not fatigue you, mademoiselle?"

"What has it all to do with me, however?" asked the lady.

"You shall hear. Though the heroine comes on late, she brings the house down when she enters. For a few weeks my patron fulfilled his compact with tolerable punctuality, but I never failed to notice when we met that he was a prey to some terrible grief. At last, when he had reduced the sum to two thousand, five hundred, and forty-three francs—the figures will be found graven on my heart—he con-fided in me, he made me a strange request; he exclaimed:—

" 'Tricotrin, I am the most miserable of men!'

" 'Poor fellow!' I responded. 'It is, of course, a woman?'

" 'Precisely,' he answered. 'I adore her. Her beauty is incomparable, her fascinations are un-paralleled, her intelligence is unique. She has only one blemish—she is mercenary.'

" 'After all, perfection would be tedious,' I said.

" 'You are a man of sensibility, you understand!' he cried. 'Her tastes have been a considerable strain on my resources, and in consequence my affairs have become involved. Now that I am in difficulties, she is giving me the chuck. I have implored and besought, I have worn myself out in appeals, but her firmness is as striking as her other gifts. There remains only one chance for me—a letter so impassioned that it shall awake her pity. *I,* as I tell you, am exhausted; I can no longer plead, no longer phrase, I am a wreck. Will you, as a friend, as a poet, compose such a letter, and give it to me to copy?'

"Could I hesitate? I drove my pen for him till daybreak. All the yearnings of my own nature, all the romance of my fiery youth, I poured out in this appeal to a siren whom I had never seen, and whose name I did not know. I was distraught, pathetic, humorous, and sublime by turns. Subtle gleams of wit flashed artistically across the lurid landscape of despair. I reminded her of scenes of happiness— vaguely, because I had no details to elaborate; the reminiscences, however, were so touching that I came near to believing in them. Mindful of her solitary blemish, I referred to 'embarassments now almost at an end'; and so profoundly did I affect myself, that while I wrote that I was weeping, it was really true. Well, when I saw the gentleman again he embraced

me like a brother; 'your letter was a masterpiece,'
he told me; 'it has done the trick!'

"Mademoiselle, I do not wish to say who he was,
and as you have known many celebrities, and had
many love-letters, you may not guess. But the
woman was you! And if I had been a better business
man, I should have written less movingly, for I
recognised, even during my inspiration, that it was
against my interests to reunite him to you. I was an
artist: I thrilled your heart, I restored you to his
arms—and you had the two thousand, five hundred,
and forty-three francs that would otherwise have
come to me! Never could I extract another sou
from him!"

As Tricotrin concluded his painful history, Mlle.
D'Esterre seemed so much amused that he feared
she had entirely missed its pathos. But his misgiving
was relieved when she spoke:

"Well, I appear to have been expensive to you,
monsieur," she said, "and you have certainly had
nothing for your money. Since this revue—which I
own that I have merely glanced at—is the apple of
your eye, I promise to read it with more attention."

A month later "Patatras" was produced at La
Coupole after all, and no one applauded its performance more enthusiastically than the poet, who subsequently went to supper arm-in-arm with its
creators.

"Mon vieux," said the elated pair, "we will not ask again by what means you accomplished this miracle, but let it teach you a lesson. To-night's experience proves that nothing is beyond your power if you resolve to succeed!"

"It proves," replied Tricotrin, "that D'Esterre's first impression was correct, for, between ourselves, my children, 'Patatras' is no shakes!"

Nevertheless, Lajeunie and Pitou wore laurels in Montmartre; and one is happy to say that their fees raised the young collaborators from privation to prosperity—thanks to D'Esterre's attractions—for nearly three weeks.

XVI

THE FAIRY POODLE

THEY were called "The two children" because they were so unpractical; even in bohemia, where practicality is the last virtue to flourish, their improvidence was surprising; but really they were not children at all—they had been married for three years, though to watch their billing and cooing, you would have supposed them to be bride and bridegroom.

Julien and Juliette had been in love and run to the Mairie as joyously as if chateaubriands were to be gathered from the boughs in the Jardin Des Buttes-Chaumont; and since then their home had been the studio under the slates, where they were often penniless. Indeed, if it had not been for the intermittent mercies of Madame Cochard, the concierge, they would have starved under the slates. However, they were sure that the pictures which Julien painted would some day make him celebrated, and that the fairy-tales which Juliette weaved would some day be as famous as Hans Andersen's. So they laughed, and painted and scribbled, and spent their money on bonbons, instead of saving it for bread; and when they had no dinner, they would kiss each other, and say, "There is a good time coming"; and they were called "The two children," as you know.

But even the patience of Madame Cochard was taxed when Juliette brought back the poodle.

She found him—a strayed, muddy, unhappy little poodle—in the Rue de Rivoli one wet afternoon in November, and what more natural than that she should immediately bear him home, and propose to give him a bath, and adopt him? It was the most natural thing in the world, since she was Juliette, yet this Madame Cochard, who objected to a dog on her stairs as violently as if it were a tiger, was furious.

"Is it not enough," she cried, "that you are the worst tenants in the house, you two—that you are always behindhand with your rent, and that I must fill your mouths out of my own purse? Is a concierge an Angel from Heaven, do you think, that you expect her to provide also for lost dogs?"

"Dear, kind Madame Cochard," cooed Juliette, "you will learn to love the little creature as if it were your own child! See how trustfully he regards you!"

"It is a fact," added Julien; "he seems to take to her already! It is astonishing how quickly a dog recognises a good heart."

"Good heart, or not," exclaimed the concierge, "it is to be understood that I do not consent to this outrage. The poodle shall not remain!"

"Be discreet," urged Juliette, "I entreat you to be

discreet, for your own sake; if you must have the whole truth, he is a fairy poodle!"

"What do you say?" ejaculated Madame Cochard.

"He is a fairy poodle, and if we treat him ungenerously, we shall suffer. Remember the history of the Lodgers, the Concierge, and the Pug!"

"I have never heard of such a history," returned Madame Cochard; "and I do not believe that there ever was one."

"She has never heard the history of the Lodgers, the Concierge, and the Pug!" cried Juliette. "Oh, then listen, madame! Once upon a time there were two lodgers, a young man and his wife, and they were so poor that often they depended on the tenderness of the concierge to supply them with a dinner."

"Did they also throw away their good money on bonbons and flowers?" asked Madame Cochard, trying her utmost to look severe.

"It is possible," admitted Juliette, who was perched on the table, with the dirty little animal in her lap, "for though they are our hero and heroine, I cannot pretend that they were very wise. Well, this concierge, who suffered badly from rheumatism and stairs, had sometimes a bit of temper, so you may figure yourself what a fuss she raised when the poor lodgers brought home a friendless pug to add to their embarrassments. However——"

"There is no 'however,'" persisted Madame

Cochard; "she raises a fuss, and that is all about it!"

"Pardon, dear madame," put in Julien, "you confuse the cases; we are now concerned with the veracious history of the pug, not the uncertain future of the poodle."

"Quite so," said Juliette. "She raised a terrible fuss and declared that the pug should go, but finally she melted to it and made it welcome. And then, what do you suppose happened? Why, it turned out to be an enchanted prince, who rewarded them all with wealth and happiness. The young man's pictures were immediately accepted by the Salon— did I mention that he was an artist? The young woman's stories—did I tell you that she wrote stories?—became so much the fashion that her head swam with joy; and the concierge—the dear, kind concierge—was changed into a beautiful princess, and never had to walk up any stairs again as long as she lived. Thus we see that one should never forbid lodgers to adopt a dog!"

"Thus we see that they do well to call you 'a pair of children,'" replied Madame Cochard, "that is what we see! Well, well, keep the dog, since you are so much bent on it; only I warn you that if it gives me trouble, it will be sausages in no time! I advise you to wash it without delay, for a more deplorable little beast I never saw."

Julien and Juliette set to work with delight, and

after he was bathed and dry, the alteration in the
dog was quite astonishing. Although he did not
precisely turn into a prince, he turned into a poodle
of the most fashionable aspect. Obviously an
aristocrat among poodles—a poodle of high estate.
The metamorphosis was so striking that a new fear
assailed his rescuers, the fear that it might be dis-
honest of them to retain him—probably some great
lady was disconsolate at his loss!

Sure enough! A few days later, when Sanquereau,
the sculptor, called upon them, he said:

"By the way, did I not hear that you had found a
poodle, my children? Doubtless it is the poodle for
which they advertise. See!" And he produced a
copy of a journal in which "a handsome reward" was
promised for the restoration of an animal which
resembled their protégé to a tuft.

The description was too accurate for "the children" to deceive themselves, and that afternoon
Juliette carried the dog to a magnificent house which
was nothing less than the residence of the Comtesse
de Grand Écusson.

She was left standing in a noble hall while a
flunkey bore the dog away. Then another flunkey
bade her follow him upstairs; and in a salon
which was finer than anything Juliette had ever
met with outside the pages of a novel, the Countess
was reclining on a couch with the poodle in her
arms.

"I am so grateful to you for the recovery of my darling," said the lady; "my distress has been insupportable. Ah, naughty, naughty, Racine!" She made a pretence of chastising the poodle on the nose.

"I can understand it, madame," said Juliette, much embarrassed.

"Where did you find him? And has he been well fed, well taken care of? I hope he has not been sleeping in a draught?"

"Oh, indeed, madame, he has been nourished like a beloved child. Doubtless, not so delicately as with madame, but——"

"It was most kind of you," said the lady. "I count myself blessed that my little Racine fell into such good hands. Now as to the reward, what sum would you think sufficient?"

Juliette looked shy. "I thank you, madame, but we could not accept anything," she faltered.

"What?" exclaimed the Countess, raising her eyebrows in surprise, "you cannot accept anything; how is that?"

"Well," said Juliette, "it would be base to accept money for a simple act of honesty. It is true that we did not wish to part with the dog—we had grown to love him—but, as to our receiving payment for giving him up, that is impossible."

The Countess laughed merrily. "What a funny child you are! And, who are 'we'—you and your parents?"

"Oh, no," said Juliette; "my parents are in heaven, madame; but I am married."

"Your husband must be in heaven, too," said the Countess, who was a charming woman.

"Ah," demurred Juliette, "but although I have a warm heart, I have also a healthy appetite, and he is not rich; he is an artist."

"I must go to see his pictures some day," replied the Comtesse de Grand Écusson. "Give me the address—and believe that I am extremely grateful to you!"

It need not be said that Juliette skipped home on air after this interview. The hint of such patronage opened the gates of paradise to her, and the prospect was equally dazzling to Julien. For fully a week they talked of nothing but a visit from the Comtesse de Grand Écusson, having no suspicion that fine ladies often forgot their pretty promises as quickly as they made them.

And the week, and a fortnight, and a month passed, and at last the expectation faded; they ceased to indulge their fancies of a carriage-and-pair dashing into the street with a Lady Bountiful. And what was much more serious, Madame Cochard ceased to indulge their follies. The truth was that she had never pardoned the girl for refusing to accept the proffered reward; the delicacy that prompted the refusal was beyond her comprehension, and now that the pair were in arrears with their rent again, she put no bridle on her tongue.

"It appears to me that it would have been more honourable to accept money for a poodle than to owe money to a landlord," she grunted. "It must be perfectly understood that if the sum is not forthcoming on the first of January, you will have to get out. I have received my instructions, and I shall obey them. On the first day of January, my children, you pay, or you go! Le bon Dieu alone knows what will become of you, but that is no affair of mine. I expect you will die like the babes in the wood, for you are no more fit to make a living than a cow is fit to fly."

"Dear Madame Cochard," they answered, peacefully, "why distress yourself about us? The first of January is more than a week distant; in a week we may sell a picture, or some fairy tales—in a week many things may happen!" And they sunned themselves on the boulevard the same afternoon with as much serenity as if they had been millionaires.

Nevertheless, they did not sell a picture or some fairy tales in the week that followed—and the first of January dawned with relentless punctuality, as we all remember.

In the early morning, when Madame Cochard made her ascent to the attic—her arms folded inexorably, the glare of a creditor in her eye—she found that Juliette had already been out. (If you

can believe me, she had been out to waste her last
two francs on an absurd tie for Julien!)

"Eh bien," demanded the concierge sternly,
"where is your husband? I am here, as arranged,
for the rent; no doubt he has it ready on the mantelpiece for me?"

"He is not in," answered Juliette coaxingly, "and
I am sorry to say we have received disappointments.
The fact is there is something wrong in the construction of a story of which I had immense hopes—it
needs letting out at the waist, and a tuck put in at the
hem. When I have made the alterations, I am sure
it will fit some journal elegantly."

"All this passes forbearance!" exclaimed Madame
Cochard. "Well, you have thoroughly understood,
and all is said—you will vacate your lodging by
evening! So much grace I give you; but at six
o'clock you depart promptly, or you will be ejected!
And do not reckon on me to send any meal up here
during the day, for you will not get so much
as a crust. What is it that you have been buying
there?"

"It is a little gift for Julien; I rose early to choose
it before he woke, and surprise him; but when I returned he was out."

"A gift?" cried the concierge. "You have no
money to buy food, and you buy a gift for your
husband! What for?"

"What for?" repeated Juliette wonderingly.

"Why, because it is New Year's Day! And that reminds me—I wish you the compliments of the season, madame; may you enjoy many happy years!"

"Kind words pay no bills," snapped the concierge. "I have been lenient far too long—I have my own reputation to consider with the landlord. By six o'clock, bear in mind!" And then, to complete her resentment, what should happen but that Julien entered bearing a bouquet!

To see Julien present Juliette with the roses, and to watch Juliette enchant Julien with the preposterous tie, was as charming a little comedy of improvidence as you would be likely to meet with in a lifetime.

"Mon Dieu!" gasped Madame Cochard, purple with indignation, "it is, indeed, well that you are leaving here, monsieur—a madhouse is the fitting address for you! You have nothing to eat, and you buy roses for your wife! What for?"

"What for?" echoed Julien astonished. "Why, because it is New Year's Day! And I take the opportunity to wish you the compliments of the season, madame—may your future be as bright as Juliette's eyes!"

"By six o'clock!" reiterated the concierge, who was so exasperated that she could barely articulate. "By six o'clock you will be out of the place!" And to relieve her feelings, she slammed the door with such violence that half a dozen canvases fell to the floor.

"Well, this is a nice thing," remarked Julien, when she had gone. "It looks to me, mignonne, as if we shall sleep in the Bois, with the moon for an eiderdown!"

"At least, you shall have a comfy pillow, sweetheart," cried Juliette, drawing his head to her breast.

"My angel, there is none so soft in the Elysée! And as we have nothing for déjeuner in the cupboard, I propose that we breakfast now on kisses."

"Ah, Julien!" whispered the girl, as she folded him in her arms.

"Ah, Juliette!" It was as if they had been married that morning. "And yet," continued the young man, releasing her at last, "to own the truth, your kisses are not satisfying as a menu; they are the choicest of hors d'œuvres—they leave one hungry for more!"

They were still making love when Sanquereau burst in to wish them a Happy New Year.

"How goes it, my children?" he cried. "You look like a honeymoon, I swear! Am I in the way, or may I breakfast with you?"

"You are not in the way, mon vieux," returned Julien; "but I shall not invite you to breakfast with me, because my repast consists of Juliette's lips."

"Mon Dieu!" said Sanquereau. "So you are

broke? Well, in my chequered career I have break-fasted on much worse fare than yours."

At this reply, Juliette blushed with all the bashful-ness of a bride, and Julien endeavoured to assume the air of a man of the world.

"Tell me," he said; "we are in difficulties about the rent—have you by chance a louis that you could lend me?"

Sanquereau turned out his pockets, like the good fellow he was, but he could produce no more than a sou. "What a bother!" he cried; "I would lend you a louis if I had it as readily as a cigarette-paper, but you see how I am situated. On my honour, it rends my heart to have to refuse."

"You are a gallant comrade!" said Julien, much touched. "Come back and sup with us this evening, and we will open the New Year with a festivity!"

"Hein? But there will be no supper," faltered Juliette.

"That's true," said Julien; "there will be no supper—I was forgetting. Still—who knows? There is plenty of time; I shall have an idea. Perhaps, I may be able to borrow something from Tricotrin."

"I shall be enchanted," responded Sanquereau; "depend on my arrival! If I am not mistaken, I recognise Tricotrin's voice on the stairs."

His ears had not deceived him; Tricotrin appeared with Pitou at this very moment.

"Greeting, my children!" they cried. "How wags

the world? May the New Year bring you laurels
and lucre!"

"To you also, dear Gustave and Nicolas," cried
"the children." "May your poems and your music
ignite the Seine, and may Sanquereau rise to eminence
and make statues of you both!"

"In the meantime," added Sanquereau, "can either
of you put your hands on a few francs? There is a
fine opening for them here!"

"A difference of opinion exists between ourselves
and the landlord," Julien explained; "we consider
that he should wait for his rent, and he holds a
different view. If you could lend us fifteen francs,
we might effect a compromise."

The poet and the composer displayed the lining of
their pockets as freely as the sculptor had done, but
their capital proved to be a sou less than his own.
Tears sprang to their eyes as they confessed their
inability to be of use. "We are in despair," they
groaned.

"My good, kind friends!" exclaimed Julien, "your
sympathy is a noble gift in itself! Join us in a little
supper this evening in celebration of the date."

"We shall be delighted," declared Tricotrin and
Pitou.

"But—but—" stammered Juliette again, "where
is it to come from, this supper—and where shall we
be by supper time?"

"Well, our address is on the lap of the gods,"

admitted Julien, "but while there is life there is hope. Possibly I may obtain a loan from Lajeunie."

Not many minutes had passed before Lajeunie also paid a visit to the attic. "Aha," cried the unsuccessful novelist, as he perceived the company, "well met! My children, my brothers, may your rewards equal your deserts in 1908—may France do honour to your genius!"

"And may Lajeunie be crowned the New Balzac," shouted the assembly; "may his abode be in the Champs Elysées, and his name in the mouth of all the world!"

But, extraordinary as it appears, Lajeunie proved to be as impecunious as the rest there; and he was so much distressed that Julien, deeply moved, said:—

"Come back to supper, Lajeunie, we will drink toasts to the Muses!" And now there were four guests invited to the impracticable supper, and when "the children" were left alone they clapped their hands at the prospect.

" How merry we shall be!" Julien exclaimed; "and awhile ago we talked of passing the night in the Bois! It only shows you that one can never tell what an hour may bring forth."

"Yes, yes," assented Juliette, blithely; "and as for the supper——"

"We shall not require it till nine o'clock at the earliest."

"And now it is no more than mid-day! Why, there is an eternity for things to arrange themselves!"

"Just so! The sky may rain truffles in such an interval," said the painter. And they drew their chairs closer to the fire, and pretended to each other that they were not hungry.

The hours crept past, and the sunshine waned, and snow began to flutter over Paris. But no truffles fell. By degrees the fire burnt low, and died. To beg for more fuel was impossible, and Juliette shivered a little.

"You are cold, sweetheart," sighed Julien. "I will fetch a blanket from the bed and wrap you in it."

"No," she murmured, "wrap me in your arms—it will be better."

Darker and darker grew the garret, and faster and faster fell the snow. "I have a fancy," said Juliette, breaking a long silence, "that it is the hour in which a fairy should appear to us. Let us look to see if she is coming!"

They peered from the window, but in the twilight no fairy was to be discerned; only an "old clo" man was visible, trudging on his round.

"I declare," cried Julien "he is the next best thing to your fairy! I will sell my summer suit and my velvet jacket! What do I want of a velvet jacket? Coffee and eggs will be much more cheerful."

"And I," vowed Juliette, "can spare my best hat easily—indeed, it is an encumbrance! If we make

Madame Cochard a small peace-offering, she may allow us to remain until the morning."

"What a grand idea! By this means we shall provide ourselves with a night's shelter and the means to entertain our friends as well! Hasten to collect our wardrobe, mignonette, while I crack my throat to make him hear. Hi, hi!"

At the repeated cries the "old clo" man lifted his gaze to the fifth-floor window at last, and in a few minutes Julien and Juliette were kneeling on the boards above a pile of garments, which they raised one by one for his inspection.

"Regard, monsieur," said Julien, "this elegant summer suit! It is almost as good as new! I begin to hesitate to part with it. What shall we say for this elegant summer suit?"

The dealer fingered it disdainfully. "Show me boots," he suggested, "we can do business in boots."

"Alas!" replied Julien, "the only boots that I possess are on my feet. We will again admire the suit! What do you estimate it at—ten francs?"

"Are you insane, are you lunatic?" returned the dealer. "To a reckless man it might be worth ten sous. Let us talk of boots!"

"I cannot go barefooted," expostulated Julien. "Juliette, my Heart, do you happen to possess a second pair of boots?"

Juliette shook her head forlornly. "But I have a hat with daisies in it," she said. "Observe, monsieur, the delicate tints of the buds! How like to nature, how exquisite they are! They make one dream of courtship in the woods. I will take five francs for it!"

"From me I swear you will not take them!" said the "old clo" man. "Boots," he pleaded; "for the love of God, boots!"

"Morbleu, what a passion for boots you have!" moaned the unhappy painter; "they obsess you, they warp your judgment! Can you think of nothing in the world but boots? Look, we come to the gem of the exhibition—a velvet jacket! A jacket like this confers an air of greatness, one could not feel the pinch of poverty in such a jacket. It is, I confess, a little white at the elbows, but such high lights are very effective. And observe the texture—as soft as a darling's cheek!"

The other turned it about with indifferent hands, and "the children" began to realise that he would prove no substitute for a fairy after all. Then, while they watched him with sinking hearts, the door was suddenly opened, and the concierge tottered on the threshold.

"Monsieur, madame!" she panted, with such respect that they stared at each other.

"Eh, bien?"

"A visitor!" She leant against the wall, overwhelmed.

"Who is it?"

"Madame la Comtesse de Grand Écusson!"

Actually! The Countess had kept her word after all, and now she rustled in, before the "old clo" man could be banished. White as a virgin canvas, Julien staggered forward to receive her, a pair of trousers, which he was too agitated to remember, dangling under his arm. "Madame, this honour!" he stammered; and, making a piteous effort to disguise his beggary, "One's wardrobe accumulates so that, really, in a small ménage, one has no room to——"

"I have suffered from the inconvenience myself, monsieur," said the Countess graciously. "Your charming wife was so kind as to invite me to view your work; and see—my little Racine has come to wish his preservers a Happy New Year!"

And, on the honour of an historian, he brought one! Before they left she had given a commission for his portrait at a thousand francs, and purchased two landscapes, for which a thousand francs more would be paid on the morrow. When Sanquereau, and Lajeunie, and Tricotrin, and Pitou arrived, expecting the worst, they were amazed to discover "the children" valsing round the attic to the music of their own voices.

What *hurras* rang out when the explanation was forthcoming; what loans were promised to the guests, and what a gay quadrille was danced! It was not until the last figure had concluded that Julien and Juliette recognised that, although they would be wealthy in the morning, they were still penniless that night.

"Hélas! but we have no supper after all," groaned Julien.

"Pardon, it is here, monsieur!" shouted Madame Cochard, who entered behind a kingly feast. "Comment, shall the artist honoured by Madame la Comtesse de Grand Écusson have no supper? Pot-au-feu, monsieur; leg of mutton, monsieur; little pâtés, monsieur; dessert, monsieur; and for each person a bottle of good wine!"

And the justice that was done to it, and the laughter that pealed under the slates! "The children" didn't forget that it was all due to the dog. Juliette raised her glass radiantly:

"Gentlemen!" she cried, "I ask you to drink to the Fairy Poodle!"